BLACK CATS' CURSE

Running from your witch,
and crossing paths with a lonesome soul,
causes a bodily switch.
That's how you'll pay the toll.

BeSwitched

Molly Snow

Published by Breezy Reads 2011

Book 1 in The BeSwitched Series

Library of Congress Control Number: 2011943252

ISBN: 0975978462

ISBN-13: 978-0-9759784-6-7

BeSwitched is a fun fairytale. It's not only an excellent read, but teaches some life lessons along the way.
— *Samantha LaSparta, Antioch Press*

ONE

Surla licked the padding to a front paw with her pink Velcro tongue. She was sitting comfortably on a winding mahogany stairway, cleaning herself after devouring another fat rat.

Click… click… click… click… Surla heard the echo of Idis's black leather boots against the floors of the Victorian mansion.

"Stay out of my way!" The witch swooshed a broom's old bristles at the back of the cat.

"Me-ow!" Surla ran and leaped to the living room's front windowsill, where pale green paint was peeling and cool air filtered in from the ajar window. Her velvety tail slinked around her little body as she peered past the porch to a quaint home across the street.

As she sat, she thought, tracing back through the three hundred years of knowing Idis. Almost every memory was horrible. She tried hard to think of a really happy time, but she couldn't. From the very moment she was taken from her mother as a kitten, and handed over to Idis as a gift from the coven at the witch's Lucky Thirteenth Birthday Bash, Surla had been mistreated.

The old witch's temper was becoming harder to handle. Her face was even becoming worse to look at. Wildly flaming red hair framed green eyes that seemed to glow just a bit. Surla wasn't sure if it was just her imagination, but it definitely seemed like her beak nose was growing with time. The only good aspect of her appearance was that she could pass for thirty-five with a lean body and smooth skin, while her sister Gretchen appeared at least three times as old.

Surla's pondering stopped immediately when she spotted the white and fluffy kitty from across the street coming outside in the arms of its elderly owner. The old lady steadied herself with a free hand to sit down on the porch's high-back, maple rocking-chair. The cat nuzzled against her crocheted shawl. Faint words trailed to Surla's ears as the owner spoke lovingly to her pet. "You are a good kitty, Diamond. A very good kitty." A knobby hand stroked Diamond's little chin and the chair began to rock.

Idis could sense Surla's envy as she was able to many times before. After taking off a boot and clipping a couple dingy toenails on a green velvet couch, she called for her cat's attention. "Help me make a fire, you lazy beast! I'm cold!"

Surla narrowed her yellow eyes in anger. She was angry because no matter what the weather, it never satisfied Idis. *She's even cold on a fresh October afternoon like today.* Surla watched the gold and yellow leaves and how they would pile together along the street and then suddenly blow away into their separate journeys.

Now it may sound as if Idis has more power over Surla, but that's not true when it comes to magic; Surla has more power. The witch just merely recites a rhyme while it is the cat's job to cast the spell. That's why you never see a witch without its "familiar" close by.

"Well?!" Idis widened her green eyes in frustration. "Get over here! What are you waiting for?"

Surla glanced at her, then back at the open window. "I don't need you," she spoke, like all black cats can do.

"So, you are dreaming about leaving again?" Idis stood, pulled down her short, black dress and grabbed for the broom. "This will teach you a lesson!" She aimed to whack Surla, but missed.

Automatically, the cat jumped through the opening in the window and over a Hydrangea bush with tremendous speed.

"Get back here, you dreadful beast!" Idis's head poked through the window in rage. "Remember the Black Cats' Curse! If you cross a human's path!" She drew in her head and slammed down the window. The bang echoed across the neighborhood, causing Diamond to leap out of her owner's arms, fur standing straight up.

Surla ran without stopping, without looking back for even a second, through the empty streets. FREEDOMMM, in her mind she screamed in silly delight. AT LAST, FREEDOM!

At that moment, Cathy, an extremely shy teenage girl with brown hair and a navy blue cardigan sweater, was walking with her head down, hoping to get further and further from the three biggest snobs from school. This was a constant routine of hers almost every day. Living in the same neighborhood as them made it so they had to take the same way home. Cathy always tried to detract as much attention away from herself as possible, but it was never possible with Tiffany, Chrissy, and Lisa around.

Much whispering could be heard. Tiffany, the ravishing blonde, was the first to say an out-loud rude comment about Cathy, as usual. "Look at how she dresses."

"It's awful," Lisa, with long black hair, remarked. "She doesn't even wear makeup. I bet her mommy says she's still too young."

The third girl, Chrissy, with a brunette bob hair-do, responded hesitantly, "Actually, you guys, she doesn't look so bad."

"What planet are you from?" Tiffany shook her head. "Sometimes I wonder about you, Chrissy."

Sometimes I wonder about her, too. Cathy remembered back to last year, her Sophomore year at Washington High. One day while Cathy was eating some french fries alone in the cafeteria, the snobs were sitting a table away with their jock boyfriends they had at the time. Tiffany stirred up a conversation about the Chess Club's president, Dwayne Dorksky, being a perfect match for Cathy. After that, a rumor was spread that the two were going together as boyfriend-girlfriend. Cathy was so embarrassed that whenever Dwayne passed by, her face would turn bright pink. Dwayne took that as a signal of blushing, so it wasn't hard for Tiffany to persuade him to ask Cathy out on a date. Being nice, Cathy slowly accepted. Months passed where Dwayne's long, gangly legs followed her everywhere around school as he attempted to flirt and hold her books. The whole saga finally ended when Chrissy told him it wasn't Cathy who was interested in him, but Jane Farnklestein, the Science Club treasurer; which was true. What a relief that was. And Dwayne and Jane have been together ever since, all thanks to Chrissy.

It wasn't a minute longer when the sound of a roaring engine caught Cathy's attention. A red sports car was nearing the girls from behind. Shiny chrome reflected sunlight, making Cathy squint.

Slowly it came to a stop next to the snobs. When the driver's side window rolled down, Cathy saw Craig Nelson, the guy she had been crushing over for two years straight.

Sure there were plenty of cute guys attending Washington High, but maybe what made Craig so alluring was how unattainable he seemed to Cathy. The people who hung around him were everything she wanted to be: popular, good-looking, and sought after for many dates. *He is just a year older than me, a Senior. That's a good thing*, Cathy thought, *because maybe someday Craig will get to know me and maybe like me for some crazy reason.*

"Tiffany, do you and Lisa need a ride home?" His blond hair was blowing back slightly from the wind as he smiled.

Chrissy looked at her two friends, disappointed he didn't mention her. Tiffany saw this and turned back to Craig. "Can Chrissy get a ride home, too? She just lives a couple houses down from me." Her voice was sweet and syrupy, so how could he say no?

"I guess there's room." His voice was smooth.

Cathy wished it was her he stopped for, but knew that was never actually going to happen, so she continued walking. *At least Tiffany won't be behind me anymore.*

"I'm sorry, Craig," Tiffany said, placing her bag in the back seat. "If Chrissy didn't come with us, then she could've been stuck walking with her." She pointed to Cathy.

Cathy felt angry and hopeless. *What can I do about it? Nothing.* The car fiercely sped around the corner, almost running into a tired black cat.

"Poor thing!" She jogged over to it as it sat there frozen, shocked. "Are you al-" Cathy couldn't finish her sentence. A weird sensation flowed through her body, making her unable to speak. She stared at the cat who sat hallow-eyed. Cathy was afraid. *Why can't I move?* Then, the feeling left and she was looking up *at herself.*

"Idis warned me of this." Cathy saw her own lips move, and heard her own voice speak.

"What? What just happened?" Cathy felt small and looked down, spotting fur and paws. "I'm a *cat*!"

"Shhh!" Surla, now in Cathy's body, said. "Calm down. You don't want anyone to hear you."

"To hear me? But I'm a cat—how can I talk? But I hear myself talk. What is going on?!" She got frantic and wiggled her tail in amazement. "Am I dreaming? Did I fall and knock myself out cold in the middle of the street?" Her new yellow eyes opened wide. "What if someone from school sees me laying in the middle of the road..." She shook from fear. "Or even worse—I could get run over!"

"Shhhh!" Surla picked her up in her arms. "You are not going to get run over. I know this looks unreal, but it's true.

5

You aren't dreaming. We crossed paths and now we're switched."

"What do you mean? It can't be!" But she looked into her own, former, icy blue eyes and knew something about it was true. "It feels so real."

"It is real…"

"Are you telling me that the saying 'It's bad luck to cross paths with a black cat' is true?"

"Yes, well, with a witch's black cat."

"A witch's black cat!"

"Shhhhh!" Surla glanced around, hoping no one was in earshot. It was a quiet community full of old homes.

Cathy lowered her voice finally. "How do we fix this?"

"By finding Idis's Spellbook."

"Idis is your witch, I suppose." Cathy was sure she was in some episode of The Twilight Zone. "Well, let's go get the book."

"No!" Surla was more afraid of seeing Idis than to be human the rest of her life.

"No? No?" Cathy jumped out of Surla's hold. "What are you talking about? We need to!"

"Not yet, anyway." Surla's new forehead wrinkled. "I'm sorry, it's just that my life is so terrible. We can't switch back until we know it's safe. Who knows what Idis will do to me if she finds me? She could really put me in danger. Please!" She knelt down to Cathy. "You don't understand how it is to live with a witch."

"This is crazy. Completely crazy."

"Listen to me. There is nothing else we can do about it. Do you really want to put us both in danger? It might take a little while, but we'll get through this."

With Surla's reasoning, Cathy calmed down, knowing there wasn't anything they could do about the situation at the moment. "This is just so weird. Are you sure I'm not dreaming?"

Surla laughed, showing a pretty smile. "I guess this would seem weird for a human. Trust me, though, everything will be back to normal before you know it."

"Normal for me isn't so wonderful." She thought of how lonely her last couple years had been since her cousin moved away.

"Why do you say that?" Surla reached carefully for her taken-over cat body, to bring her safely to the sidewalk, and with fright Cathy's new black ears flattened back for the first time.

"The fact is…," she sighed, and continued, "that my life is a total bore! I'll probably be nineteen before I get a boyfriend and as far as Craig Nelson goes, I'll probably never get him."

"Who's Craig?"

"He was in the car that almost ran you over." Her tail twitched. "He was driving."

"Why didn't he give you a ride?"

"Me?" Cathy looked down. "I'm not popular enough. Craig doesn't even know I exist."

"Well, I don't know why." Her new fingers combed through her hair. "You have very silky hair. I'm sure I can get him to notice you."

"Oh no!" She remembered something else. "What do we do when we get to my house? My mom's expecting me soon."

"It's simple. I pretend I'm you and ask if I can have you as a pet."

"Purrfect," Cathy practiced.

"And when's dinner?" Surla licked her lips. "I've been starving for another fat rat."

"Disgusting!" Cathy said. "You are not going to ever put some nasty rodent into my mouth. You are human now, so you eat human food. Now, follow me." She headed in the direction of her house.

As soon as they reached the small, yellow home, with a peach tree in front, they headed into the garage from a side door. Inside, they quietly discussed their plan. "I only live with my mom." Cathy sat on the washing machine. "My parents divorced a few years ago."

"So, you weren't raised with a litter of brothers and sisters?" Surla worked at buttoning her cardigan sweater with a little difficulty.

"Uh… no."

"Neither was I. At least, from what I remember." She smiled. "There is this one cat I call 'cousin,' but he is really annoying."

"I have a cousin, but she lives in Kentucky." Cathy paused. "But, anyway, you better hurry and get inside. Just watch some TV, and then at dinnertime bring up the idea of having me as a pet. She is most happy while she's eating."

"So am I." Surla laughed. "This will be simple. A dog could even do this." She headed to the door to the kitchen.

"Don't turn out the lights," Cathy said fast. "It's bad enough I have to stay in here so long with spiders who knows where."

TWO

Idis was becoming more and more frustrated as the day wore on. She began uttering words under her breath as she tromped around the neighborhood. "That horrid cat! Horrid, horrid, horrid, horrid."

The sun was setting a pale orange and the wind was picking up; a typical night for October.

The witch's green, glowy eyes leaped from one spot to the next in desperation. "When I catch you, you'll have even less freedom than you had before. You'll live in an itty bitty cage for the rest of your nine lives." Her back hunched over as if it would bring her closer to finding Surla, when suddenly, a rustling was heard around a couple of tin garbage cans.

"Aha!" she whispered, rubbing her palms together. "Could that be you, Surla, hiding from me?"

Her orange-lipsticked smile stretched in exaggeration as she tip-toed over to the noise. She was able to spot a movement underneath an old newspaper. Idis crouched down on her knobby knees, placing her face above it. The paper then shook as if it was afraid.

Her long fingers approached it, ready to grab whatever was underneath.

The witch's movements were quick and precise. The paper was scooted off and a brown, dirty rat was taken in both her hands. It squeaked and Idis dropped it, instantly shaking from head to toe. "Eeww, nasty rat. I hate rats!"

Idis ran until reaching the inside of her kitchen, where she spent time washing her hands until they were red. "Next time it won't be any rat, Surla!"

Cathy was nervous as she heard voices and movements from inside the kitchen. She knew it was dinnertime and hoped that Surla would have good manners and bring up the subject of having her as a cat easily. *What would we do if my mom said no to the idea?*

Surla stared at all of the food placed in front of her. There was a fresh green salad, mashed potatoes with gravy, and some chicken. *The chicken looks good*, she thought. She was nervous once Cathy's mom took her place across from her. She wasn't sure how much food to take and how to properly eat it.

"Sorry I was so late coming home, but the post office needed me, since Jackie was sick," Cathy's mom said, while taking some chicken.

Surla noticed, besides the resemblance between the mother and daughter, a nametag on her work uniform that said Julie Phillips. *Whatever you do,* Surla noted, *do not call her Julie; she is 'Mom.'*

"So, how was your day at school?" Julie continued, reaching for the salad.

"Oh, it was fun." Surla smiled.

"Fun?" She arched an eyebrow. "How well did you do on your History test?"

Surla had to think quick. *What if Cathy had done bad on the test?* "I did better than I thought I would." She was happy with her response.

Surla looked down at her empty plate, with blue flower designs. She could smell the inviting aroma of all the food in front of her, especially the chicken. Very rarely Surla was allowed to go outside, when living with Idis, so it had been a long time since she last tasted a bird. She was eager to eat it, but focused on not showing that eagerness too much as she reached for a thigh, then looked across the table for a lead to follow for manners.

"Cathy, is something wrong?"

"No, why?" Surla unknowingly gave a funny grin.

"You just don't seem like yourself tonight."

That's because I'm not, she thought. "I-I've just been thinking a lot today and I was wondering if I could have a pet."

"A pet? What, a dog?" Julie started eating her chicken with her fingers.

"No way!" she exclaimed. "I mean, I would rather have a cat. One that's black with yellow eyes."

"Oh?" Cathy's mom walked to the refrigerator and brought out a pitcher of juice. "It's just that, the way you're always petting Sadie, from next door, I thought you wanted a dog." She poured herself a cup. "But... I don't know, Cathy. I'm going to have to give it some thought."

Right then, a crash was heard from inside the garage. Cathy had fallen asleep from waiting so long and rolled off of the washing machine, hitting some unsteady boxes. She sat there still, hoping they didn't hear from inside. The thought of hiding came to her immediately, but the idea of being crammed in a cobwebby corner made her stay where she was.

"What was that?" Julie looked up, afraid, setting down her drink.

"I don't know." Surla acted undisturbed.

"It came from the garage." She walked toward the door, wiping her hands off along the way.

Surla knew there was nothing she could do. "Mom" was going to find out about her plan before it even was situated and Surla hoped she would be understanding. She watched her slowly turn the doorknob, opening the door just a bit. "The light is on... I didn't leave it on," Julie whispered, frightened.

"I must've left it on." Surla walked over, pushed open the door, and stepped in.

"Meeow." Cathy tried to sound natural.

"Oh, look, *Mom*—a cat." Surla leaned down and picked her up.

"That's no ordinary cat. It's a black one with yellow eyes... like the one you asked for."

"I'm sorry, I saw it on my way home from school, hungry and without a collar. It was a stray. I couldn't just leave her."

Surla is a good talker, Cathy thought as she saw her mother's expression change considerably.

"Isn't she adorable?" Surla persuaded more.

"Well, you said she was hungry, didn't you?" Julie took Cathy and pet her.

"Yes." Surla smiled.

"Go inside and get her a couple chicken strips then." She sat on the hood of a broken-down station wagon.

"Okay." Surla was ecstatic and rushed inside. *It worked*, she thought.

"I can be such a pushover sometimes." Cathy's mom laughed lightly. Surla soon returned having Cathy eating out of her hands.

"So, what should we name her?" Julie asked.

"You mean... we can keep her?!" Surla's new blue eyes were bright with excitement.

"I suppose." A half-smile came across her lips.

"Thank you so much, um, *Mom*!"

"Well, what name do you have in mind for her?"

"Su-" She stopped suddenly rethinking that using her real name would not be such a good idea. What if Idis were to hear it being called throughout the neighborhood? "S-Sadie sounds good."

"But, Cathy, you don't want it to have the same as our next door neighbor's dog!"

"Oooh! Of course not! What am I thinking?"

"Licorice?" Julie suggested after a while.

"I like it. It sounds sweet." Surla was happy and so was the rest of her new family. *My new family*, she repeated in her head. That sounded nice to her, however temporary it would be.

Cathy was still tired and shut her eyes. She soon awoke in the arms of Surla, taking her to her bedroom. Once inside, Surla closed the door. Cathy jumped onto her large bed.

Surla took a long look around the plain room. It was almost colorless. A dresser in the corner held only a lamp and picture of Cathy with her mom. The most interesting spot was her window, which had long curtains; they were silky and rose-patterned, like what a grandma would prefer.

In the closet, Surla shuffled through long skirts, cardigan sweaters, silk blouses, and a couple pair of tennis shoes. *What a boring assortment*, Surla thought. *There's just no magic in it.*

"Your life will be different for the time I'll be in your body, Cathy." Surla closed the closet door and sat next to her sleepy friend.

"Yeah, well, I'll be glad to get a break." She breathed in slowly. "Tomorrow is Saturday, my favorite day of the week because I have no school."

"What's school like?" Surla sprawled out.

"For me, it's not fun at all." She yawned, curling her tongue. "If you're like Tiffany and her friends, then you have a blast, getting boyfriends constantly and going on dates with popular guys like Craig."

"What's Craig like?"

"He is hot." A purr started. "The best water polo player, with the best body. I've adored him for two years straight—since ninth grade. We have had a couple classes together, but we never spoke a word to each other. It's like I'm invisible to him." She paused. "I can't believe he and Tiffany haven't gotten together yet. If I could just get him to notice me and ask me out on a date, it would be a dream come true."

"If you like him that much," Surla said, "I'll get him for you."

"Sure you will." Cathy's eyelids felt heavier. "Can you turn out the light and go to bed now?"

"All right." Surla stood, hit the switch, and curled up on the bottom of the bed.

THREE

"That's most of my baby-sitting money you're using to get my nails done!" Cathy hopped onto her dresser, where Surla scattered money out of a wallet. It was early the next morning and Cathy's mom had already left for work.

"I'm sorry, but your nails are in bad shape. You must have bit them every time you got bored." She counted out about twenty dollars. "I have pride in keeping mine long and sharp."

"Well, forget about the sharpness," Cathy said, then counted what was left of her cash. "I only have fifteen bucks left!"

"Good." Surla snatched it up. "I can buy you a collar and leash with that."

"A leash? I am not a dog!"

"We can't be too safe." Her new blue eyes opened wide. "If Idis sees me, who knows what will happen."

Cathy thought it over. "I guess you're right."

"And of course you aren't a dog." Surla laughed. "You're too clever."

Surla put on a pair of blue jeans and borrowed a navy blue turtleneck from her new mom's wardrobe. Soon they left with money to spend, on a bus headed toward the nearest mall.

Surla opened the door to leave the pet shop. Cathy walked ahead of her, wearing her new red collar and matching leather leash. She wriggled her head back and forth feeling it around her neck. *It's not too bad*, Cathy thought. *It's kinda like wearing a choker.*

Inside Shelley's Nail Salon, it smelled strong of chemicals from the two different manicurist's stations. One lady, with brown hair and bright pink lipstick, was already busy gossiping with a customer while giving her a french manicure. The other was sitting, reading a popular magazine. Her blond, curly hair was put up wildly in a ponytail. The two were into what they were doing so much, they didn't even hear the bell when the door was opened.

Surla walked slowly over to the blonde, who finally looked up from her reading. Her eyes were a sassy brown, accentuated even more by black eyeliner. It reminded Surla of a cat.

"Hi! My name is Patricia, but you can call me Patty. What can I do for you today?" She stood, showing off how short and petite she was.

Surla cleared her throat. "I came to get my nails done, because I've been biting them a lot lately and now I want to grow them out."

"Sure. I could do whatever style you want." She then glanced down at Cathy.

Surla noticed this and said politely, "Oh, I'm sorry. Do you think my cat, Licorice, can stay in here with me? I don't want to let her out of my sight." She looked down to see Cathy rubbing her head against Patty's ankles.

"Oh, Okay." She smiled. "As long as my boss isn't here. She won't distract you, by like jumping on your lap while I'm working on you, will she?" Patty sat in her chair.

"Don't worry," Surla assured her, "Cath… I mean, Licorice, is a well behaved cat."

"I hope you're right." She laughed and organized her tools before starting.

Outside, at a nearby park, Revere Park, Idis was becoming more clever than frustrated. A pile of papers were clenched in her hands. She had a plan. Today, she was dressed like the rest of society. Her flaming-red hair was placed as neatly as possible into a french twist. Her dress was black, but longer than usual and didn't cling to her body as much. She even wore some spectacles; there wasn't much she could do about her beak-like nose they sat on though.

"Excuse me." Idis almost choked on such proper words. She had stopped a man with an obvious toupee, carrying a briefcase. His cheeks were pudgy and his beard looked maybe three days old.

"Yes?" He was taken aback, looking at her nose in awe.

"Here." Idis shoved a paper in his free hand. It had a crayon drawing of Surla on it. "Have you seen this cat? It's mine and it ran away."

He looked down and smiled at it. The picture looked as if a five-year-old was the artist. It was clear that it was black with yellow eyes, which was probably good enough.

"Sorry." His eyes went straight to her nose again. "I haven't seen any black cats around lately. I'm a very busy man. I'm going to the bus stop, so I can get to work now. Good luck." He chuckled, walking off. "I wouldn't even notice if my wife brought home a cat."

"Yeah, well, I hope you have a rotten day, too," Idis muttered.

Back at Shelley's Nail Salon, Patty was filing Surla's new red nails. Surla couldn't keep her eyes off of Patty's eyeliner. It appealed to her catty taste.

"Your eyes are so pretty," Surla finally said as her thumb was being worked on.

"Thanks," she said modestly. "It took me a while to learn how to do my makeup nice. Without it, I look like an owl." She finished filing. "Is this a good shape for you?"

Surla spread her fingers, looking at the rounded shapes. "Can you make them more pointed?"

The manicurist gave her a funny look while Cathy (sitting on Surla's lap) nudged her stomach in disapproval. "Are you sure?" Patty asked.

"Yes, I'm sure," Surla said. "I want them all sharp…er, more or less.

"Oookay." She took her file and worked hesitantly.

Surla spent two hours preparing for her first day of high school. She put her brown hair into a high ponytail, wore blue jeans, and a tight black top borrowed from Cathy's mother again. Her icy blue eyes were lined like Patty's, making them appear sapphire. Lastly, Cathy prepared her with the list of classes and a backpack to put all her books inside.

Once Surla was walking through the halls of Washington High, a surge of excitement went through her body. A day that Cathy dreaded, Surla was anticipating. *I wonder who I'll make friends with*, Surla thought as she looked at all the many different faces of teenagers, all shapes, sizes, and races. What surprised her the most was mostly all eyes were on her—at least the guys' were anyway.

Heads were turning everywhere. One guy was staring at her so much so, he accidentally walked right into a pole; he paused for a second, startled, and then went on staring as if nothing happened. *I sure am attracting a lot of attention.* Surla was amazed.

The school was bigger than she expected also. She saw many steps, halls, courts for playing basketball and tennis, a football field, and a theater for acting.

The bell rang, startling Surla. She pulled her wadded up schedule out of her pants pocket. *First, I have History*, she read, *in room 509. Where is that?* She saw the closest classroom door said 218. *Oh no, it will take me forever to find this class.*

Students were rushing to their classes with their friends. Surla felt overwhelmed. *Just keep walking*, she told herself. *You'll find it eventually.* She couldn't let anyone know she wasn't sure of the demographics to the school she had supposedly attended for the last two years.

She continued down the hall and turned the corner, almost bumping into a tall, dark-haired guy, wearing a red letterman jacket.

"Cathy?!" His surprised, green eyes opened wide, looking Surla up and down.

"Yes." She smiled, wishing she could call him by name also.

"Wow, you look so… different." He smiled back.

Who are you? she wanted to say.

"Why are you going this way?" He laughed. "History is in the opposite direction."

Thank goodness. He must have class with me. I can follow him. "Oh, I know. I was just…" She was at a loss for words. "Never mind."

She went with him across the quad to another building of classes. *If this is Craig*, Surla thought, *then Cathy has good taste.*

"Come sit by me," he said, leading her to a desk in the back. Once again, Surla noticed all the staring eyes.

"Oh my gosh!" said the girl sitting on the opposite side of her, covering her mouth. She was a cute girl with big brown eyes and a matching bob hair-do.

At that exclamation, a blond girl turned in her seat to look. She was pretty with pouty lips. "Wow, she's wearing makeup," she said with the least amount of excitement as possible. "Well, it's about time. I think she heard us Friday when we were talking about her."

"Tiffany!" the other girl said disapprovingly.

"What, Chrissy?" She lifted her eyebrows. "What's with you? You're so 'goody-goody' sometimes. And don't give me that attitude."

That definitely has to be the snobby Tiffany, Cathy was telling me about, Surla remembered. *It's about time Cathy talks back, instead of being the same timid mouse she always has been.* "Excuse me," Surla said to Chrissy.

"Yeah?" Chrissy said hesitantly.

"Did she just say you were the one with the attitude?" Surla made sure she was loud enough for Tiffany to hear.

"Yes."

"That's very funny, coming from her."

Surla could see Tiffany breathe in deeply. Tiffany then turned around to say, "Stay out of my and Chrissy's business."

Surla looked to her left to see that the guy wasn't in his seat. She glanced around the room and quickly spotted him sharpening his pencil. Surla took the opportunity to growl behind Tiffany's back, "Reeeow." If she had her other ears, they would have been flattening to her head. Then, she smiled at Chrissy. A smile crept on Chrissy's face also, as she unsuccessfully tried to hold back laughter.

Tiffany, once again, turned in her seat, this time looking Chrissy straight in the eyes. "I know you are not laughing at me, because *nobody* laughs at me."

By this time the guy had returned to his seat next to Surla. "Hi, Todd," Tiffany said, smiling.

"Hey, Tiffany." He smiled back, then grabbed his backpack to pull out a binder.

So, that's not Craig, Surla realized. *He's cute though… for a human.*

A short, balding man with glasses approached the front of the classroom. "Okay, everyone, you know the drill. Pass your homework assignments up to the front row."

Bags and binders were shuffled through, including Surla's, but she couldn't find any homework for History. The teacher noticed Surla's confusion and walked over to her desk. "Where's your assignment, Cathy?"

"I'm sorry. I was really busy this weekend, so I don't think I got it done."

"This isn't a class to slack off in. Remember the grade you received on your last test?"

She knew by the tone in his voice, it must have been really bad. "Yes. I'm sorry."

His face lightened up a bit. "Okay, then I expect you'll do better next time."

Do better next time? Surla was worried. *But what do I know about History?* Then she quickly reconsidered. *Hey, it's not like I was born yesterday. I'm not sixteen years old like Cathy.* Her mind backtracked to the time she and Idis lived in Salem, Massachusetts—where the witch trials were held.

FOUR

"She's a witch! She's a witch! She's a witch!" the crowd chanted.

Idis stood at the accused stand, with Surla at her feet. A fat, balding man, who reminded Surla of the History teacher, took his seat as the judge.

"All right, everyone!" his voice boomed. "Just quiet down! We'll find out soon enough if this lady here is a witch!"

"Just look at her nose!" A man in his twenties, wearing a farmer's hat, pointed.

"And that black cat!" a plump lady, holding a baby, shrieked.

"Yeah!" The crowd started up again.

"Now, settle down!" The judge stood, waving his arms. "If you settle down, this will be over with all the sooner."

Instantly the crowd became quiet. The only noise heard was by a lady's baby, who was now crying.

"Okay, Idis," he began, "are you a witch or aren't you?"

Idis was on the verge of a nervous breakdown. Her hands shook and beads of sweat started running down her forehead. Surla became very worried for her own life. Whatever they would do to Idis, they were sure to do to the cat. If Idis was going to be burned at the stake, then so would she.

"Well, are you?" The judge pushed for an answer.

"No," she finally stated firmly.

In response, the crowd became more heated with anger. "Liar! Liar! Liar!"

"All right. All right! I *am* a witch!" she screamed in rage. "And now I'm going to cast a spell on all of you!"

Surla was horrified. *Is she crazy?!* she thought.

The crowd gasped and became silent. Some ran and ducked away. Surla felt she had to do something and fast, so she jumped onto the judge's lap, purring and rubbing her head against him. *The point is for me to look as sweet and innocent as possible,* she thought, *so I look like I am not a witch's black cat. Besides, if I don't agree in using my magic, then Idis's spell won't work.*

Idis threw her arms straight up in the air and yelled, "Shoooraca shum! Mewoka reds! Make everyone this instant have bald heads!" Her head fell back in hysterical laughter, but she soon noticed no one was losing hair. She tried again, but it still didn't work. Maddened, she stomped her feet. "Bald heads, I said!"

Everyone looked around, feeling their hair, followed by a roar of laughter.

"It's too late, Idis." The judge rubbed his already balding head. "You don't scare me. Ladies and gentlemen!" He chuckled. "Oh boy, I guess we came to our conclusion." He paused to pet Surla. "Good kitty." Then he looked up again at Idis. "I find this lady not guilty of witchery, but guilty of craziness! So, on behalf of Salem, Massachusetts, I sentence you and your cat to a mad house… or to leave our town. Oh, I guess the kitty can stay if it wants."

"Cathy… Cathy." Surla's mind slowly came back to History class, as she felt a tapping on her arm.

"Oh… um, yeah?" She turned to Todd.

"The teacher has been trying to get your attention."

"Oh." She smiled in embarrassment.

"I don't believe you've listened to a word I've said so far." The teacher set down his book. "Cathy, what could you possibly be daydreaming about that is more exciting than History?"

"Actually," she laughed, "I was thinking about History."

"Cathy, pay attention." He eyed the room, spotting a guy with long hair, resting his head on the desk. "James!"

"H-huh?" He looked up, his eyes tired.

"No sleeping in my class."

After that, Surla tried really hard to pay attention or at least pretend to pay attention, but anything that came out of the teacher's mouth sounded like a bunch of blahs. Blah... blah... blah... blah, and soon the bell rang to go to the next class.

"Hey, Cath." Todd finished packing his bag. "What were you really daydreaming about?"

"History." She half-laughed.

"Oh." He looked puzzled. "Well, I guess I'll see you in Chemistry."

"Okay." Surla smiled, watching him leave as she pulled out her schedule again. *P.E.*, she read. *I hope I'll have luck finding it.*

Back at the house, Cathy was becoming very bored taking naps, drinking milk, and watching TV. She felt the need to get out of the house. After all, it was the sunniest day October had seen so far.

Cathy sat on a windowsill in the living room, looking out at the bright afternoon with birds chirping and people bicycling. *Wait... birds!* Cathy saw two blue jays hopping and singing on her driveway. She stared at their feathery, little bodies from a different perspective. *How fun it would be to chase one*, she thought. "Hold on, Cathy!" she told herself. "You are human, not a cat. So, think human!"

She sat there, closing her eyes, imagining she was in Craig's arms. Feeling better about herself, she opened her yellow eyes again and longingly looked outside. "Okay, so I won't chase birds. Maybe a roll in the grass would be nice, though."

With one of her paws, she pulled up the latch, to unlock the window. With the side of her small body, she pushed hard, trying to open it. It didn't work, so she tried a second time, taking a deep breath before. Again it didn't budge. Finally, she tried with full force and energy. It worked! The window went ajar a few inches, just enough for her body to slide through and skip a muddy puddle. "Whew! Third time's a charm." She pranced around the yard and rolled in the grass. "Ooh, the things we humans take for granted." The soft, cool grass tickled her back.

"Grrrr... grrr," she heard from the next yard over. Cathy remembered the black Labrador, Sadie, from next door. Cathy looked over her shoulder cautiously, and to her relief her eyes followed a silver chain hooking from its neck to a tree. Once again, she rolled in the grass.

"Grrrowl! Grrrowl!" Sadie kept on while the chink of the metal leash was heard.

Don't worry about her, she comforted herself. *Just keep rolling.*

"Rruff! Rruff!" Growls turned into barking and Sadie leaped, even though she was restrained.

"Rrrruff!" The sound of metal snapping like a twig, startled Cathy.

Cathy turned in horror as she saw the slobbery beast darting for her, the broken chain sliding on the ground.

"AAAAAH!" she screamed and took off to the side yard, where she ran between some garbage cans full of aluminum. Sadie didn't care; she ran straight through, causing cans to fly in all directions.

Cathy turned, while still running, noticing the bear-like claws coming closer to her tail. She felt as if her heart was going to leap right out of her furry chest. *This was the dog I used to play with after school!*

She soon made it to the other side of the backyard, where a tall wooden fence blocked her from the front yard. *This is not good*, she thought. *Not good at all.* She then leaped as high as she could. Her front paws barely touched the top of the fence and without thinking, nails jutted out, hooking into the wood, preventing her from falling. Her back paws scratched, trying to push the rest of her body up.

Sadie appeared under her in a flash, showing off her sharp teeth. Cathy felt weaker, as if the blood was being drained from her legs. But when Sadie jumped, biting for Cathy's tail, enough adrenaline rushed through her to make it back over to the front yard.

She had to sit and catch her breath. The aroma of roses her mother planted last spring was a nice, therapeutic scent. *I've got to make it back inside*, she told herself. The window left open was about ten feet away. She slinked her body like a furry snake in the grass. She was almost there, when the sound of Sadie tromping through the cans, caused Cathy to sit still in fear. Her eyes were stuck on the entrance from the side yard, expecting the dog to come out any second—and she did! Her pink nose lowered to the ground, sniffing intensely around some bushes.

Cathy looked up. She could see the opening in the window. If she was quick enough, she could make it. Sadie made it over to the peach tree and bit into one of the many fruits fallen to the ground. *I could make my move now*, Cathy thought. *Oh no!* The Labrador's black, beady eyes made eye contact with hers and the side of her lip curled with a growl.

"AAAAH!" Cathy scrambled through the muddy puddle and made it up through the window. She was safe. Wet dirty paw prints decorated the windowsill as Sadie whimpered and scratched beneath her, outside. "Down, doggy," Cathy spoke, happy and unafraid.

"What are you doing?" an old man came from the house next door, speaking to Sadie in a displeased tone. He walked over to his dog and lifted the broken chain hooked to its neck. "Bad dog! This is the second time you've done this to our neighbors." He waved a finger in disapproval.

Cathy was laughing inside.

Sadie craned her neck, looking back at the black cat, while being pulled away home; the black cat who could speak just like that Cathy-girl.

FIVE

Surla sat between rows of lockers. The smell of too much perfume and hair spray made her feel like gagging. She had found her way to P.E. and the oversized T-shirt and sweat pants, left in Cathy's locker, felt very comfortable.

Chrissy was pulling her short hair into a small ponytail in front a huge mirror hanging on a wall. Her eyes glanced at Surla's, then looked again and smiled. *Chrissy is way more nice than her friends.*

"Girls! Let's go! Time to hit the tennis courts!" a manly-looking lady with a whistle hanging around her neck, yelled.

As Surla headed out the door, Chrissy came alongside her. "Hi, Cathy," she said.

"Hi," she said back, with slight amazement that Chrissy would regard her.

"You look really nice today. You should dress like this every day."

"Thanks," Surla responded as they headed to the courts, where all the students, guys and girls, were asked to sit and form a large circle. The two teachers, Mrs. Brown (the manly lady) and Mr. Townshend (the manly man), stood in the center.

"Okay, everyone! Today is the first day of practicing tennis," Mrs. Brown began. "Tennis is a pretty simple game, but it takes a lot of sweat and stamina. Although it may seem so, it's not easy to run back and forth from one side of your court to the other trying to hit a little ball."

Mr. Townshend interjected, "Yes, and in a few minutes we will discuss the rules of the game, but first we need everyone to partner up with someone. So, hurry up and get with someone!"

Surla looked around at all of the students finding their friends. Feeling a bit uneasy, she looked at Chrissy, who she noticed didn't have a partner also.

"We'll be partners, I guess." Chrissy stretched her arms above her head.

Thank goodness. Surla smiled.

"All right, I see everyone has found their teammate, so sit close to each other so we know for sure who you're with," Mrs. Brown ordered. "And we'll go around and pick the people you're up against. And it looks like it will be an even boys against girls."

Of course all the boys were happy with that conclusion, already eyeing the girls they wanted to compete with. Surla and Chrissy listened to Mr. Townshend calling off names of who would be against who. "Steve Campbell and Byron Thompson are with Sophia Sanchez and Crystal Bradley." The teams stood up and grabbed rackets and a ball from a sports rack.

"Mr. Townshend!" Sophia whined with a cute accent. "Why did you put me with Byron? You know we don't get along at all."

"Well then, this will also be a lesson in learning to get along with others who are annoying," he said with a laugh, teasing Byron, then continued on, "Nick Costa and Patrick McNeal are up against Suzy Peters and Sara Cronopolous."

Sara ran over to Nick and gave him a high five. "All right! We're on the same court." Then they headed out with their equipment.

The pairing up of teams went on and on until Surla became anxious. "The only guys left," Chrissy whispered, "are Jason Renshaw with Paul Hadlock and Travis Simmons with Craig Nelson."

"Craig Nelson!" Surla said more excitedly than she meant to.

"Yeah, why?" Chrissy laughed. "Do you like him or something?"

Surla felt stupid for sounding so eager. "No, I don't." She then thought she really shouldn't lie about Cathy. "Well, yes, I guess I do."

"Really?!" Her big eyes became bigger with interest. "You know," she lowered her voice more, "Tiffany has had the hugest crush on him for two years in a row. Can you believe it? But don't tell anyone I told you."

"Wow… okay." Surla thought about how the situation had been the same with Cathy.

"I know. Personally I don't like any of the guys here. I guess growing up with them all made it unexciting for me, but maybe if some really good-looking new guy came to school…." Chrissy stopped and looked at the four guys sitting across from them. "Cathy," she said in an enthusiastic whisper, "Craig is staring straight at you!"

"Really?" Surla casually glanced over to him and their eyes met instantly. *This could be my first opportunity to flirt.* Surla smiled as cute as possible, tilting her head. Craig smiled back and gave her a wink.

"Oh my gosh. Did you just see what he did? He winked at you!" Chrissy looked again to Craig and then back to Surla. "I won't tell Tiffany about this one."

"Tiffany?" Surla turned to her. "Why? What can she do about it?"

"Oh, trust me, she can do a lot." Her eyebrows raised. "I've known her practically my whole life."

"You have known her almost all your life?" Surla felt sorry for her.

"Oh yeah. She just lives a few houses down from me."

"Can I ask you a question?"

"Sure. What is it?"

"Why do you hang out with her?"

"Why do I hang out with her?" she said as if the answer was obvious. "Like I said, I've known her practically all of my sixteen years. We used to play Barbie when I was just four. She's my friend, so why wouldn't I want to hang out with her."

At that comment, Surla decided not to say another word about the topic, seeing as how it would offend Chrissy.

The teacher announced, "Jason Renshaw and Paul Hadlock go with Alana Gustafson and Taniesha Collins."

Surla knew what that meant. *Yes! I'm with Craig. What a great coincidence.*

"The rest of you know who you're with," Mr. Townshend said as they stood and picked out rackets. Surla reached for the green, fuzzy ball, which appealed to her catty interests.

"Hey, what's your name?" Craig asked Surla as they all headed to a court.

Oh my gosh, Surla thought in amazement, *he doesn't recognize Cathy!*

"This is Caaathy. Can you say Cathy?" Chrissy teased.

"Cathy?" he said again. "No way! Um, what's her last name? Philbert!"

"No, it's Phillips," Surla said.

"Oh, wow." His blue eyes were glued to staring at her for a few more seconds. "Hey, um, I'm sorry I didn't give you a ride home last Friday. My car was pretty full."

"Don't worry about it." They went to their separate sides of the court. "I wouldn't want to be in the same car as Tiffany anyway."

Craig's mouth dropped open. "Man, Cathy, you've changed."

"I know." She smiled. "Isn't it great?"

The two P.E. teachers quickly went through the rules of tennis. Then all the students proceeded to play, but Surla kept throwing the ball in the air and catching it over and over.

"Okay," Travis, Craig's partner, spoke up, "you can serve it to us now, Cathy."

"Oh, I'm sorry." Surla hit the ball nicely across to the other side of the court.

For the first few games Craig and Travis won, but as the period went on Cathy and Chrissy were becoming better players, winning the last two.

The bell rang as Surla placed her and Chrissy's rackets away. Before entering separate locker rooms, Craig said to them, "You two are tough, for girls."

"You're pretty tough, too, Craig—for being a guy," Chrissy remarked.

"Well, I'll see you later." He started to walk. "Oh, and you too, Chrissy!"

Chemistry went by too slow for Surla. Even though Todd sat next her, they weren't allowed to talk. *Mrs. Spencer talks way too fast!* Surla grumbled in her head. *And why does she have to use so many words I cannot understand? All my life I've used magic. I don't want to start learning science.* She tapped her sharp, red nails on the desk lightly.

"All right, class," the very serious-faced teacher said, "your homework will be on page five-fifty-seven in the textbook. It's a review on everything we have learned in the last two weeks." She slid her wire-rimmed glasses to the top her head. "I'll see you all tomorrow."

The bell rang. People rushed out of their seats, anticipating going home.

"You looked like you were having a tough time understanding." Todd walked out of the classroom shoulder-to-shoulder with Surla.

"How could you tell?" she said.

"It was that twisted look you had on your face." He chuckled.

"Thanks." Surla smiled. "But it's not my fault. Mrs. Spencer is hard to understand. And I do not want Cath…, I mean, *my* grade to drop."

"Well, hey, Chemistry is one of my easy subjects. Maybe…," he continued as he scratched the back of his neck shyly, "I could, like, tutor you or something."

"Yeah, maybe. I'll think about it." Surla had to ask Cathy's mom if it would be all right if he came over.

"Okay." He headed toward his locker. "Don't take too long to decide."

Surla knew by instinct, the route to reaching Cathy's house again. *First, I have to go by Revere Park.* She smiled at how good the day had gone so far.

SIX

As Surla was walking home, she heard the sound of footsteps follow behind her. She turned to see Tiffany, Chrissy, and a Hawaiian-looking girl with long black hair. Chrissy smiled slightly at Surla. The two other girls started whispering.

Wind started blowing golden and brown leaves down the sidewalk. *Idis's favorite month*, Surla thought. Revere Park could be seen with its maple trees and segments of a short stone wall wrapping around it. As she was getting closer, sheets upon sheets of paper were spotted, posted on the trees. *I wonder what those could be. Maybe a big event is going to happen.* They rippled in the breeze, when suddenly one ripped loose. It flew, twisting and turning in her direction. It finally ended up face down a few feet away.

When Surla picked it up and saw what it contained, she gasped. It wasn't about an event; it was about herself! Her ice-blue eyes skimmed the horribly drawn picture of a black cat. In bold ink, at the bottom, was written, "Idis's missing cat, Surla. 713 Shadyside Street."

Chills ran through her body, as her eyes darted to the numerous fliers. *I can't let anyone see these!*

"What's the matter, Cathy?" Tiffany mocked, as she and her two friends walked ahead.

"Just keep walking." Surla wasn't in the mood to be bothered by the snob. Something more troubling was on her mind.

She hopped easily over the small stone wall, to the park, and headed to a tree with three of the same notices posted. After ripping them down, she continued gathering more. "So, so many," Surla murmured. Sheets blew all around her, twirling through the air and catching in bushes and benches. Pretty soon she held a stack of about twenty.

"Hey!" Surla recognized the growling voice from behind her as she kneeled, picking up another. Her heart skipped a couple beats when she turned to see Idis scowling at her.

"What do you think you are doing?" The frenzied witch snatched the papers out of Surla's shaking hands.

Surla brushed a flyaway strand of brown hair out of her eyes nervously. "I-I was just… collecting some?"

"What do you mean, 'collecting some'?" She copied the unsure answer.

Her glowing, pale green eyes made Surla feel as if Idis could see right through to her true identity.

"Um… uh, uh," she stammered. "Because I-I." *Stop acting like this, Surla!* she scolded herself. *If you keep this up, Idis is sure to figure it out.*

"Oh, just shut up and get out of my way!" A cold hand pushed Surla down onto a bench. She then proceeded to nail a flier to a tree with a small hammer held in her dress pocket. "I don't want to see you pick up any more of my missing cat notices. If you even had a clue as to who I am…" Idis aimed wrong, hitting her thumb. "Ouch!" she yelped, dropping the hammer on her black boot.

If only you had a clue as to who I am, Surla considered with fright. Without hesitating any longer, she hopped the wall and jogged to Cathy's home.

She entered the house through the unlocked garage door. Once in the kitchen she heard the sound of splashing water and singing. "Row, row, row your boat, gently down the streeeam!"

What is she doing? Surla quietly peeked around the corner to see the living room, where Cathy was scrubbing the wooden floors. Green sponges were hooked to each paw. "Merrily, merrily, merrily, merrily, life is but a dreeeam."

"If you're going to croon, stay in tune." Surla laughed, surprising Cathy.

"Don't scare me like that. For a second you sounded like my mother. She would have had a heart attack if she saw a singing cat!"

"What happened in here?" Surla saw a bucket of sudsy water and muddy paw prints everywhere.

"Sadie, the dog from next door, chased me all around outside and before I could jump back inside through the window I ran into a muddy puddle."

"I never did like dogs." Surla said as she grabbed a sponge from underneath one of Cathy's paws. "I'll help. It will get done quicker."

"Thanks." Cathy's skinny tail popped up suddenly. "What happened at school today? You know I've been dying for you to tell me."

"School was fun, but let me first tell something more important that happened after school." She pulled off her tennis shoes before cleaning.

"What?" Cathy stopped in interest.

"I ran into Idis at Revere Park."

"No way! An encounter with the witch?"

"Yep. And she's been really busy lately."

"What do you mean?"

"She must have over a hundred fliers about me." Surla groaned. "Maybe two hundred."

"Really!"

"Uh huh, and there's nothing I can do about it, because she threatened me when seeing that I gathered a bunch of them."

"Oh no," Cathy growled. "What if my mom sees one of those?"

"All we can do is hope she doesn't."

"You're right." Cathy continued scrubbing the floor. "What's today's *good* news?"

"Well, I saw Craig in P.E. We were on the same tennis court and he told you he was sorry for not giving you a ride home Friday."

"Oh my gosh! He did?"

"Yes." Surla laughed. "But he didn't even recognize you at first."

"He didn't?" Her voice lowered in disappointment.

"Oh, don't worry. I can tell he thinks you're cute." Surla looked down at the tight black outfit she had picked out. "Everyone thought you were. You received so many compliments and heads turning today. One compliment I know was from a guy named Todd, and then another by a girl named Chrissy."

"Chrissy and Todd?" Cathy's ears stood straight up like radars.

"Yes, why?"

"Well, it's just that Chrissy hangs out with Tiffany, the girl I told you about who I don't like at all, and Todd... well, he's that really cute quarterback of our football team."

"He is cute." Surla stopped in thought for a second. "Do you think he's cuter than Craig?"

"I don't know." Cathy sighed. They were almost done cleaning the floor. "They are about the same, but if I had to choose... I would choose Craig, of course. He just seems like a really cool guy. He can get any girl he desires."

"Well, things are starting off pretty good between you two so far." Surla finished the last dirty spot, then returned the bucket and sponges to underneath the kitchen sink.

"Hi, Cathy. Hi, Licorice." Julie came in the front door, as they were laying on the couch, exhausted by the day. She took a seat next to them exclaiming how tired her feet were.

"Hi, Mom." Surla sat up and yawned.

"I smell Pinesol." She smiled, looking at the shiny wood floors. "Thanks. I'll finish up later with some wood wax."

"No problem." Surla pulled down her high ponytail that was giving her a headache.

"Oh yeah, I almost forgot." Julie pulled a folded up piece of paper out of her pants pocket. "This was posted on our door, before I left to the post office this morning."

Cathy and Surla turned to each other. Both had apprehension spelled across their faces. They knew what was to be shown—Idis's missing cat notices.

"I just thought this was important... a Halloween party at Revere Park. There will be dancing, contests, and spooky treats." She then read straight from the notice. "This event is for both of the city's high schools to attend. They can have fun and be safe at the same time." She paused and looked up at Surla in the eyes. "Well, Cathy, what I was thinking was... you should go to this party... you know, because you aren't as social as you could be." Cathy rolled her yellow eyes as her mother continued, "You haven't had any friends over in a while... and the only person who calls is your cousin in Kentucky."

Surla thought that to be funny and grinned. Cathy on the other hand did not find it amusing at all—her right ear twitched.

Julie sat there, waiting for some response.

"I'll go." Surla smiled slightly, but inside she couldn't hold her excitement, *Oh boy, oh boy, sounds so fun!*

"Did I just hear you say you'll go to this Halloween party?"

"Yes, Mom. Don't worry, I'll go. It sounds like fun."

"Well, I'm happy I didn't have to beg."

"Oh, no. It's fine." Surla leaned over to rub her cheek against Julie's in a purr, but was grasped into a hug.

The next day at school, in a light breeze, Surla played tennis with Craig again. Everyone seemed to be having a great time, except for Chrissy. She was constantly missing the ball, even if it headed straight for her racket. The guys were ahead in points, of course, and Chrissy didn't seem to care.

What's wrong with her? She was doing so well yesterday. Why isn't she putting much effort into it today? Surla thought.

After losing all of the games to Travis and Craig, Surla ran to the corner of the court to get a drink of water. Chrissy collected the rackets and returned them to the stand. As Surla drank, Craig snuck up from behind and tickled the sides of her stomach.

"Hey!" She turned around, wiping water from off her chin.

He smiled and his blue eyes lit up. "Sorry, but you were drinking for so long, I was wondering if you were going to save any for me."

She laughed, playfully pushing his shoulder. Craig then took a quick drink and turned to Surla again. "Hey, um, can I get your number?"

My number? she thought, puzzled. "13?" *I like that number.*

Chrissy unknowingly saved her from more embarrassment by tapping her on the shoulder and saying, "Come on... Mrs. Brown is calling us. We'll be late for our next class."

"Oh, okay." Surla looked to the locker room and saw the teacher waving for them to hurry up. "Bye, Craig." Surla walked off with Chrissy.

"I guess I'll get it later then!" Craig called.

"He'll get what later?" Chrissy asked, concerned.

"Oh." Surla recalled his strange question. "He said he wanted my number." They entered the musty locker room.

"Don't give it to him." Chrissy's big brown eyes were serious.

"But why?"

Chrissy pulled her hair out of its short ponytail, then continued, "I warned you about how Tiffany likes him. Just take my advice and don't do it; don't give him your number."

Surla decided she would have to wait until after school to ask Cathy what she wanted to do about the situation. *How bad can Tiffany be?* she thought, undisturbed.

In Chemistry, Surla sat next to Todd again, since he saved a seat for her. Mrs. Spencer was at the front of the class, giving another one of her hard-to-understand lectures. Everyone was expected to write notes, and that's exactly what Todd and Surla did, except they were writing them to each other.

Using his elbow, Todd passed the paper onto her side of the long lab desk they shared. Surla glanced down and read: *You look really nice today, just like you did yesterday.*

She had chosen to wear a navy-blue turtleneck, from Julie's closet. Her hair was down this time, with the ends curled from rollers, and her eyes were once again emphasized by the black liner.

She wrote back in loopy letters: *Thank you. You look really nice also.*

His dark hair was styled neatly and when he read her response he smiled, showing dimples. He wrote back: *Have you decided if you want me tutoring you after school?*

Surla had completely forgotten to ask Cathy's mom if it would be all right. *I really need the help though. Especially since there will be a test soon!* Remembering that, she had made up her mind: *Yes, I have thought about it and decided I would like you to help me.*

She pushed the note over, and he quickly jotted down: *Great! I'll teach you about Chemistry, while we make some of our own :0)*

Surla had a good idea of what he meant by that. *I'm not supposed to be attracting you. I'm supposed to be attracting Craig,* she thought. So, she wrote: *Let's just stay with the dictionary's definition of Chemistry, for now.*

After class, Surla let him know that tomorrow would be good for him to come over. She needed time to tell Cathy and her mom about it first.

This time, when walking home, Tiffany, Lisa and Chrissy were ahead of Surla. Tiffany wore a red cotton dress that, according to the wind's direction, blew to and fro along with her hair. She had to admit, Tiffany was a very pretty human. *Perhaps a little too thin*, she thought; *but, very pretty, nonetheless.*

Her eyes then scanned over to Lisa. Her black hair was incredibly long, reaching passed her rear in a thick braid. Her figure was cute; she was petite.

Surla noticed Chrissy's brown hair actually had some red highlights in it. She wore a turtleneck, like Surla today, but it was black. All three of them together made an incredible sight.

HONK! HONK! A red sports car pulled up alongside the girls. Tiffany smiled brightly as the driver's window rolled down. Craig's blond hair was blowing back with the breeze. "Hi, Tiffany. Hi, Lisa. Hi, Chrissy."

No 'hi' for me! Surla stopped in her tracks.

"Hey, Craig." Tiffany walked over to him with books in her hands. "I'll just throw my stuff in the back." She waved over her two friends.

"Actually," Craig stopped her, "I think I owe someone else a ride." His eyes looked to Surla and she smiled.

Tiffany glanced around. "Who?" she said as if she was oblivious to Surla's presence.

"Cathy." He called her over with the wave of a hand.

"Her?" the snob said in disgust. "Well, fine. That's all right, because I'm getting my license soon and won't need a ride home anymore." She turned around sharply, pulling Lisa's arm. "Come on."

Surla waved bye to Chrissy as she entered the sports car; but, in response the girl just shook her head, then kept walking with her friends.

Craig took off, speeding as usual. "So, where do you live?"

Surla had to jog her memory for the street names. "Oh yeah, Spaulding Way off of B Street."

He laughed. "Did you almost forget where you live?"

"No… it's just, never mind." She had no good answer.

"You always walk home?" he asked like he already knew the answer.

"Yes." Surla looked in the rear view mirror at the three girls turning into dots, then disappearing in the distance. "Tiffany looked pretty mad back there."

"She'll live. Sometimes she can really get on my nerves." He turned on some rock music.

"She gets on my nerves all the time," Surla said as he turned a corner almost reaching Cathy's house. "It's that house with the peach tree in front."

He came to a stop in front of the small home. Before she opened her passenger-side door, Craig's warm hand reached for hers. "Wait," he said and she turned in her seat, seeing him smile softly, "if ever you need a ride, just ask. The weather is getting colder and colder." His hand still held hers. "Oh, and I guess you can just give me your number when you feel comfortable."

She would have given it to him right then if she knew what he was talking about. "Thanks a lot, Craig." Surla opened the door and he gave her hand a squeeze before letting go.

As soon as she entered the house, Cathy was at her feet all bright eyed. "What just happened? I saw you exit Craig's car!"

"Cathy, Cathy, Cathy, Cathy." She picked her up and cradled her in her arms. "First, I want to know how you knew that?!"

"If you must know, I am stuck here all day by myself watching talk shows, napping, or perched on a windowsill watching birds." She was slightly embarrassed of her quick confession. "Anyway, while looking out the window, I saw you drive up in his car—Craig's car! So, pleeeeease hurry and tell me what happened."

"Okay," she said, self-satisfied. "I've been hooking him by my cat-like ways."

"Tiffany, this is not fair," Chrissy said, still walking home with her and Lisa. "What has she ever done to you?"

"Look, Chrissy," Tiffany said with much conceit, "Cathy is trying to ruin my reputation… and I'm not going to let her get away with it."

"No, she's not," Chrissy defended. "She's just finally coming out of her shell."

"All these years, I have been the girl who guys go crazy for. I am not going to let some geek-gone-gorgeous steal that away from me," she said matter-of-factly. "She deserves whatever's coming to her."

"My phone number is 555-9145." Cathy showed Surla the buttons on the cordless phone. "Okay, the phone is to talk to people that are far away. You talk into it and they talk back through their phone. You can hear each other."

"Ooh! I saw your mom using it last night and was wondering what she was doing." Surla laughed.

"I can't believe Idis didn't have one of these."

"Well, she had something like this. She got in contact with other witches through a mirror."

"Now, that sounds a little too much like a fairy-tale to me."

"A little too fairy-tale-like, huh." Surla tilted her head. "How would you describe our situation?"

"Okay, you win."

"Mirror, mirror, on the wall, who is the fairest one of all?" Idis contorted her body into the sexiest move she could make, in front of a full length mirror. Black iron wound around it in a gothic manner. "Well?!" she yelled at it for an answer.

"I'm sorry, Idis," the congenial deep voice said, "I'm not in the mood to play Snow White." The glass swirled with changing colors.

"Oh well," the witch grunted, "what I really wanted to do was call up my sister, Gretchen."

"Gretchen?" he repeated. "All right." Sounds of dialing started. Then slowly coming out of a blue fog, a tall beautiful woman in a bikini appeared with a seascape rolling behind her.

"Yes, Vladimirror?" the woman purred.

"Who are *you*?" Idis's neck protruded like an angry chicken. "You sure aren't my sister!"

"Oops," the mirror chuckled in embarrassment. "I must have hit redial."

"Well, Vladimirror, I see what you do in your spare time. Now get Gretchen!"

"Okay, okay." There was a series of beeps, like more dialing, and this time out of a green fog, a short, frumpy witch appeared. She wore layers of old clothing and her red hair was stringy. "Well I'll be a good witch!" She cackled sarcastically. "You haven't called me up in ice ages, Idis! You must have some crisis going on."

"Gretchen, I need you to do a favor for me," Idis choked out.

"A favor from *me*?" She cackled some more. "What's wrong? Did your cat finally run away?"

"Yes!" she yelled, stomping her boot's sole on the floor.

"Well, what do you want from me…? To build a fire, to clip your toenails?" Gretchen paused, then continued, "Oh, that's not possible. Your toenails are probably harder than a tooth!"

"That's not true." They argued like children. "I just clipped them last week!" Idis took a deep breath in to calm herself. "I, uh, was wanting to know if I could borrow your cat."

"Ha ha! Little *Pus*face wouldn't want to spend a minute with you. Besides, how would I do my magic without him?"

"It will just be for a little while. I need him to help me find Surla."

"Why, that's impossible." Gretchen placed her pudgy hands on her hips. "You know if my cat goes out there hunting for yours, then it can become BeSwitched."

"No, remember the Black Cats' Curse only applies if your cat runs away. Pussface will be helping me, not running away."

"Oh yes, how could I forget?" She stood in thought for a moment. "What would I get out of this?"

"Well, Vladimirror can hook you up with The Witches' Home Shopping Network."

"Hmmmm." Gretchen rubbed her hands together. "That sounds like a deal. You know I enjoy collecting junk." Right then a scruffy black cat was tossed into Idis's arms.

"Bye," Idis called.

"Bye, bye. I'll be waiting for my shopping network." Her sister disappeared in the green fog.

"Hey, you didn't ask me if I wanted to hook the shopping network up for her," the mirror whined.

"Don't feel too bad," Pussface commented. "At least you aren't exchanged with other witches without being asked."

"Hush up, you mangy critter." Idis dropped him to the floor of her bedroom. "You are going to help me find Surla no matter how you feel."

"I kinda figured that already."

Surla couldn't believe two weeks had already passed. Time was flying faster than anticipated. Being a human was becoming second nature to her and tomorrow would be the last day for playing tennis in P.E. Every two weeks they would learn a new sport.

Surla had planned on making all the flirtatious moves on Craig, but he ended up making them all on her. Before playing, he asked if he could get her phone number again. Chrissy and Travis had to wait while he got a pen to write it on his forearm. "555-9145," he repeated.

"Yes." Surla smiled, now knowing this was a major step in gaining a relationship.

When she returned to her side of the court, Chrissy shook her head in disapproval. Surla had not forgotten the warning about Tiffany, but she felt that intimidation shouldn't stop her from helping Cathy's situation. Whenever Surla scored a point, Craig would wink at her. Sometimes it even seemed as if the points were given to her, especially since Chrissy wasn't putting in full effort again. And she could see how annoyed Craig's partner was becoming, for letting her and Chrissy win.

When it was one of Craig's turns to serve, he moved his eyebrows up and down at Surla before whacking the ball. The ball whirled in the air and Surla tried to reach it with her racket, but it was too far away. Instead it went flying toward Chrissy.

Chrissy was looking at her nails.

"Watch out!" Surla called, but it was too late. The ball knocked her on her forehead.

"I'm sorry. Are you okay?" Craig ran over to the net.

"Yeah, I'm fine." She rubbed the red spot and shot him a fiery look. Surla knew it must have hurt, but that didn't seem like a good enough reason to be angry.

"It was an accident," Surla told her.

Chrissy dropped her racket and went to the corner of the court. "Tell Mrs. Brown I'm hurt if she asks why I'm sitting out."

"I'm really sorry," Craig said once more.

She must be mad for more reasons than the fact that the ball hit her in the head, Surla concluded. Craig and Travis began bouncing the ball off the wall, while Surla went to the corner to talk.

"What?!" Chrissy said, pestered.

46

"So, what's been going on? Why have you been acting like this for the last couple of days?"

"Acting like what?"

"Come on, Chrissy. What's wrong?"

"Nothing." She sighed.

"Whenever people say 'nothing' it usually means 'something.'" Surla sat down. "You can tell me. Does it have to do with Tiffany?" she said, lowering her voice.

"It's about Craig and Tiffany. I told you already, she likes him."

"I know, but if Craig likes me then I should go for him. I don't think he likes her."

Chrissy sat, watching the guys still hit the ball off of the cement wall. "I understand how you feel, Cathy." She looked Surla straight in the eyes. "But I don't think you understand what Tiffany is capable of doing. I'm sure she could get Craig right now or talk him into anything."

"Then why hasn't she done it yet?" Surla played with the draw-string to her sweats, not bothered by Chrissy's warning.

"I don't know." She shook her head.

"Why isn't this court playing tennis?" Mr. Townshend yelled to them. Instantly they all went to their spots, even Chrissy. This time Travis served the ball.

In Chemistry, Surla reran the conversation she had with Chrissy over and over in her mind. *Should I be afraid of Tiffany?* she seriously considered.

Todd passed a note to Surla with his elbow, which said, *What's wrong?*

I just have a lot on my mind, she wrote back.

Do you still want me to come over today?

That question conjured a guilty feeling, because she still didn't get around to asking Cathy or her mom if it would be okay to have Todd over. *Of course I still want you to come over*, she wrote anyway.

Good!!! I was hoping you'd say that.

Do you have a car? Surla desperately didn't want to walk home.

Todd's truck was a dark blue. The interior had brown, leather seats, which Surla liked the most. When she sat down it was nice and cushiony. The feeling reminded her of how soft her fur used to feel.

As they drove by Revere Park, Todd pointed out Tiffany, Lisa and Chrissy. "I used to like Tiffany."

That didn't surprise Surla. "Didn't every guy at one time like her?"

He smiled, but didn't answer.

Surla stared a minute noticing his nice profile. His nose was perfectly sloped and his eyebrows were dark and shaped around alluring green eyes. But she thought his cheekbones were the most attractive; they stood out, making him look more masculine or older than the other boys at school.

"What are you looking at?" He smiled and turned to her a second.

"You."

"I know. I saw you out of the corner of my eye." Todd laughed.

"Then why did you ask?" she teased.

Right then, a roaring engine was heard. A red sports car zoomed by and Surla caught sight of three girls sitting three-in-a-row in the back seat: a blonde, a brunette and a black-haired beauty. She knew exactly who they were. *Didn't Craig say Tiffany can get on his nerves?* Surla remembered the conversation she had riding home with him just yesterday.

Cathy was perched up on the windowsill, as usual, watching birds go by. She liked it especially when the feathery creatures would land. To see them hopping around on the concrete made her excited, even yearning to go out and play. She had no intention of eating one, just playing, but no way would she leave the house after what happened with Sadie the other day.

"I had a boring life as a human, and now I'm having a boring life as a cat." Cathy said to herself. Her ears twitched at the thought. "Oh well, that's why Surla's working to help me out."

Soon after, she saw a shiny blue truck with tinted windows pull up to the curb.

"Who could that be?" She squinted her yellow eyes, trying to see through the windows, but it was no use. The passenger side door opened to reveal a pretty girl with a high ponytail. "Surla!" She was happy and anxious, wondering what happened to her at school today.

Surla grabbed her backpack and stepped out onto the lawn. Then, the top of a guy's head was revealed as he came out of the driver's side. He had dark hair. "That's not Craig, so who is it?" Cathy said right before Todd appeared, walking next to Surla. "Todd?! Why's he coming over? Oh my gosh… how do I look?" She started running toward a mirror, but stopped short. "You idiot. You're a cat. You always look good… cuddly and cute," she told herself.

SEVEN

"Your cat is so cuddly and cute," Todd said as he held Cathy in his lap, stroking under her chin.

"Isn't she?" Surla took that compliment for herself. She opened her Chemistry book as they sat on Cathy's bed.

Cathy felt nice having a guy hold her. It was the first time ever. That realization made her feel a bit sad, but then she just focused on his fingers running down her back and forgot about it. Without trying, she began to purr and imagined Todd was Craig.

"So, what are you having troubles with?" Todd interfered with Cathy's fantasy as he took her off his lap and put the Chemistry book in place of her.

"Eeeverything," Surla said, hopeless. Science never made any sense to her. Dealing with magic all her life was much more easy.

"Okay." He lifted an eyebrow. "Why don't we take it from the top then. Open to the beginning of the chapter."

As they worked together, Cathy observed how Surla handled conversation and movements with him. So far she looked cute and comfortable. *How does she do it?* Cathy envied.

After a while, Cathy looked at the alarm clock on the small dresser beside her bed. It said 4:30. *My mom should be coming home from work soon. I don't think she would like to see me alone in my room with a boy! I have to let Surla know somehow.*

"Hang on. Repeat what you just said. I don't understand." Surla leaned looking over Todd's notes.

"Okay, you see this formula?" He pointed to a scribbled mess.

"Um, yeah, but it's kinda unclear the way you wrote it."

What do I do? Oh my gosh. Cathy tried to think of a way to get Surla's attention. "Meeow! Meeeoow!"

"Your cat sounds like it's sick." Todd looked at Cathy and rubbed her back.

"She just likes the attention." Surla's eyes were glued to the notes. "What does this say, so I can write it on my paper."

Can't she tell what am doing? Cathy became frustrated. "Meowww!" Her little black body pounced at the clock, knocking it over.

Todd laughed. "Psycho kitty. What's the matter with her?"

Finally Surla looked up to find Cathy nudging the clock with her nose.

"Ooh." Surla's mouth dropped when she noticed the time. "Oh, I think Licorice is trying to tell me it's time for you to go now."

"Your cat…," he looked at Cathy quizzically and continued, "is telling you it's time for me to go?"

"Well, uh…" Surla set the clock upright. "Some people have watch dogs; I have a clock cat." She laughed. "Look, it's 4:33 and my mom will be coming back from the post office soon. I didn't tell her you were coming over, remember?"

"Oh, okay." He stuffed his notes and books into his bag. "Well, how about you ask your mom tonight if it would be all right if I tutored you tomorrow? We didn't even get halfway through."

"Sure. This time I won't forget, I swear." They walked to the front door.

"I really liked coming over and getting to know you better. You're really interesting." He unlocked the door. "And so is your cat." Todd laughed when he saw Cathy at his feet, rubbing against his ankles.

Just then the door opened, scaring the three of them. A woman stood there with the same look on her face. "Hello?" she said, seeing Surla behind Todd.

"Mom!" Todd said. "I mean, uh, Cathy's mom." He nervously looked back to Surla. "Uh, Cathy, I-uh better be going. See ya 'round."

He started to go through the door, but an arm caught him.

I am in trouble now! Surla and Cathy thought in unison.

"What's going on here?" Julie ignored Todd's attempt to leave.

"Mom, I have an explanation." Surla forced a smile on her face while Todd brushed a hand through his dark hair. "He came over to help me with Chemistry."

"Chemistry huh?" A look of disbelief was in her eyes. "Show me your work."

"I wouldn't lie to you." Surla looked sincere, and walked to the room to get the proof where she could hear Cathy's mom talk.

"What's your name?" she heard her say.

"Todd. Todd Wilkenson."

"My name is Julie," she answered back. "My daughter is having trouble with Chemistry?"

"Yes."

"She never did before. Her problem subject has always been History."

"Really? She's been doing good in that class. I know because I have that class with her, too."

Surla rushed back to the living room with her spiral notebook. "Right here—the study of acids and bases." She pointed. "Todd has helped me a lot."

"Okay, Cathy." Julie glanced at the work. "Maybe Todd did come over and help you with Chemistry, but you still didn't ask me if it would be all right, especially since I wouldn't be here."

"I know. I forgot and I'm sorry." Surla tilted her head.

"I'm sorry, too, Mrs. Phillips," Todd interjected politely.

"Well, a sorry is nice, but you're still going to be punished for this, Cathy."

Punished? Surla was scared. *How do humans get punished? Are they not fed dinner for a couple days, like Idis did to me? Am I going to have to live in the garage? Or get hit with a broom*—she quickly looked to the kitchen, spotting the prickly, yellow devil that was hooked to a long stick. *A long stick to reach the victim's backside,* she knew from experience.

"Is Todd going to get punished also?"

"I'm serious." Julie reopened the front door. "You won't be able to see my daughter out of school for about a week," she spoke to the apologetic young man. "If you still want to help my daughter, then you can do it in the school library."

"All right." Todd left, waving bye to Surla. Soon after the door was shut, his dark blue truck was heard leaving.

"Cathy!" Julie's voice raised considerably since a stranger had left the house. "What were you thinking? Letting a boy over without my consent!" she continued, barely taking in a breath. "You thought you would just sneak him in and out before I came home, didn't you?" It looked as if Julie's eyes would never blink again. She paused, then walked off to her room flustered. "And you heard me when I said you are grounded this whole week!"

Surla sighed deeply. "I messed up…"

EIGHT

"Excuse me." Pussface approached Diamond, the fluffy, white cat from across the street. His own fur was patchy; where some spots were full it wasn't far from other spots that were close to bare, like around his neck. The Marilyn Monroe of all felines turned her head, eyeing the homely black cat.

"Listen, I know only black cats can speak, but you can be of great help to me if you would just nod or shake your head in response to questions I'll ask you." He sat in front of her, desperate. "I'm helping my witch's sister find her missing cat."

Diamond began to lick her paw.

"The cat I am talking about is the one who lives across the street."

Diamond looked to the pale-green Victorian home with its witch's cap's sparkling stained-glass window and beat-up wrap-around-porch.

"Have you seen Surla around, maybe trying to hide out in corners… or even come over to visit you?"

She shook her head no, causing her expensive collar to glitter in the sun.

"Okay." Pussface gazed at her almost perversely. "Well, I see you're of no help to me in this area, but... if you ever feel lonely and want to go for a stroll through some ally, then just ask, Sweet Thing."

Diamond yawned and jumped onto the porch's rocking chair.

"I'll take that as a maybe." He walked off slowly. "Catch ya later."

"What is the matter with you?" Idis said to Pussface, while she tried to start a fire in the fireplace. "I send you out to do a simple task, yet you come back with no information."

"Well," Pussface scratched behind an ear, "I did find out one thing while looking through a next door neighbor's window. Did you know that humans have no fur on their butts?" Pussface's snaggle-tooth poked out in a grin. "How's *that* for some information?"

"Did you happen to be looking in a bathroom window? You nut!" She turned around sharply. "You have to take this job seriously. Surla is your cousin and my only way to perform magic."

"But there are so many places she could be... doing anything."

Idis's mouth dropped open in realization. "You are right. Absolutely right!"

"What, what did I just say that was so important? I'm confused here." He scratched behind an ear again.

"Don't you get it?" The witch smiled crookedly, not noticing the newspaper she had been using to feed the fire was flaming up wildly. "Surla could be switched at this very moment with a pathetic, lonesome soul."

"Idis, that dress is on fire!" Pussface warned.

"I know it looks great, but there's no time to bring up how beautiful I am right now. We have to think up a strategy." The burning was slowly creeping up the bottom of her short skirt.

"No, Idis. You are literally on fire. If you don't put out the flames now I'll have to put them out for you." He lifted one of his back legs like a dog.

The witch finally understood. Feeling the burning sensation, she took off running to the bathroom to douse it in the sink.

Fearing for Idis's safety, Pussface cast a spell. "Flip that witch 'round and 'round, 'til those flames are—uh—drowned!"

Idis hit the floor, flames growing. "Oh no!" she yelped, then rolled across the shaggy throw rug, back and forth, back and forth, so fast that all Pussface could see was wildly wind-milling legs and red hair. "I'm going to kiiiillll youuuuuu!"

"Should I stop this or keep it up?" Pussface laughed. "A few more seconds won't hurt her." But he did stop the magic right away.

Idis laid flat on her back, unable to speak or move.

Pussface approached her slowly. When she was no longer dizzy and her eyes could finally focus, she shot him a wicked stare.

"Idis, I was just trying to help. You know—stop, drop, and roll?"

She continued staring.

"Here, let me just... fix your hair a little," Pussface said apologetically, drawing out four claws and combing her bangs a bit.

"DON'T touch me!" She pushed him away.

"I was just trying to help."

She stood up, pulled down her dress and excused herself to the bathroom, then returned with a wet towel dabbing herself. "Broom, please."

Pussface obediently handed her the broom.

WHAP! "Now I feel better," she exclaimed.

Pussface sunk to the ground, seeing stars.

"Now, like I was saying—you stupid cat—tomorrow I want you to go house to house throughout this whole neighborhood, hiding in backyards, peeking in windows, trying to find where the girl lives who switched bodies with Surla. Got that?"

The next day of school was pretty much the same for Surla: Craig was flirty, Tiffany was snobby, Chrissy was distant, and Todd was nice even after the incident with Cathy's mom. During lunch, Todd helped Surla with her studies in the library, where Cathy's mom said they should study.

After school, on the usual walk home, Tiffany stopped Surla. "I see no one is giving you a ride home today."

"Likewise," Surla responded.

Tiffany and her two friends followed beside her. "Don't you remember me telling Craig I won't be needing a ride home from him anymore because I'm about to receive my license?"

What Surla *did* remember was seeing the back of her head in Craig's car yesterday, but she decided to say nothing. She still saw the missing cat notices posted everywhere, which was more important at the moment than Tiffany's rude comments.

"You think you're so hot these last few days, don't you?" the conceited girl kept on.

"What are you talking about?" Surla pretended to be confused. "I've always been hot."

"I wouldn't say that." She raised an eyebrow. "But recently you have come close to looking normal."

Surla stopped walking. "Listen, um, this is getting really old. You have been obsessed with bothering me for a long time now and I don't know why, but you and your friends…," she glanced at Chrissy and Lisa, "are not going to lower my self-esteem and you are not going to stop me from being who I am."

She continued to walk until she came to the intersection where they would depart. "Yeah, well…," Tiffany was searching for some last words, "you just better watch your back… because… because anything can happen. Just be ready for it."

Surla sighed and continued down her street. *She's never going to quit*, Surla thought.

Saturday morning was brighter than the usual days for fall. Rays filtered in through Cathy's curtains and onto her bed, where Surla was curled up into a ball at the bottom. She stretched, accidentally hitting Cathy with her arm, waking her also.

"That's what I thought would happen," Cathy said after yawning.

"What?" Surla asked.

"It's a beautiful day out and I'm grounded." Cathy wiped her eyes tiredly.

"Cathy, you stay at home practically all the time now. What's the difference?"

"I know. It does affect me though because I can't watch Lassie now."

"Yeah." Surla agreed. "And I can't watch talk shows."

The two then looked at each other like they were just brought out of a daydream. Cathy spoke first. "Do you think I am beginning to think like a real cat?"

"I know what you're saying. I'm feeling more human every day."

"This is scary."

"Yeah."

"D-do you think this can become permanent? Like I could be stuck as a cat for the rest of my life."

"No, it can't be," Surla answered. "If that's true, then my life span has been shortened a couple hundred years. Seriously though, I think we're just figuring out how it feels to be one another."

"How do you like it? Being me?" Cathy sat up.

"I can see how a human's teenage years can be very emotional. I've never felt so many feelings as I do now that I'm being you. I mean, before I was able to feel angry and frustrated with Idis and even envious of the cat from across the street. But…," she patted down her flyaway hair, "I never felt anticipation for tomorrow or excitement to meet new people like Todd. Most importantly, I never felt loved like what becoming a part of your family did."

"Thanks, Surla."

"For what?"

"Crossing paths with me."

NINE

Pussface had been watching people around the neighborhood for a couple of hours. He saw ordinary situations: men mowing their shaggy lawns, people riding bicycles together in unattractive Speedos, and others gardening.

"I haven't seen anything unusual so far," he muttered while passing lovely one-story homes. One had a blooming rose bush and children's toys in the yard. The toys were being played with by a little girl with blond pigtails.

"A kitty!" he heard her say. She skipped over to Pussface in her pink-striped dress. He let her pet him a minute with her chubby fingers. "Good kitty-kitty."

"Okay, I must be going now. I have business to take care of," the cat said, but before he could walk away, she picked him up, unsteadily. Half of his body dragged on the ground. The girl looked like she was of an age of believing in imaginary friends, so a talking cat didn't surprise her at all.

"Kitty-kitty, come play with me." She smiled while rubbing her head on his.

"What have I gotten myself into?" Pussface sighed as they entered the house.

"Shhh," she whispered and brought him into her bedroom. She dropped him, then closed the door quietly. "My mommy doesn't like kitties. She-she says they make hew sneeze." Like most young children, she couldn't pronounce her Rs.

"Maybe I should go then." He knew if Idis saw he was wasting time playing, she would be very angry.

"No. Just for an itty bit of time. Stay and play." The girl pulled a plastic child's table to the center of the room. She then scooted two little chairs to it. "We awe vewy phosisticated ladies." She went to her closet after placing Pussface on a chair.

"Can't I play a sophisticated *man* instead?"

"No!" she demanded and grabbed herself a big hat with a red ribbon on it. She then took a doll off the bed and began to undress it.

"What are you doing?" he asked, fearing his assumption.

"Like I said, we awe phosisticated ladies."

"How old are you?"

"Thwee." She held up four fingers.

"Okay." Just then he felt her stuffing the doll's dress over his head. "Agh! I think that's the arm-hole," he choked.

"Oops." She giggled, then put it on right, Velcroing the back together. "That looks lovely, Emily." She raised the pitch of her voice in an attempt to sound like a proper woman.

"Thanks." He looked down to the flowered pattern and puffy shoulders. "But the name is Pussface. My witch calls me Pusface, but it's Pussface."

"Okay, Emily." She sat across from him and smiled. "We awe having a tea pawty. We awe pwincesses."

"How absolutely splendid," he mimicked a woman's voice from England.

The little girl giggled and pretended to take a sip of tea out of thin air. Her pinky finger was sticking straight out.

Pussface began to follow her motion with a paw. "Where's my pinky?! Oh dear heavens, my pinky is missing!" he joked.

"Silly Emily. Isn't it a beautiful day out?" She took another imaginary sip.

"Yes, a beautiful day to play cricket. And a beautiful day to find Surla."

"What?"

"Hey." Pussface's orange eyes opened wide. "Maybe you can help me."

"Help you do what, Emily?"

"Have you seen another black cat around lately? Maybe you've had a tea party with another talking cat?"

"Nope. Just you." Her hand pet the top of his head.

"I look ridiculous in this outfit and it feels tight. I think it might be cutting off some circulation." One of his back legs was feeling a bit numb.

"You're not playing wight." Her bottom lip pouted.

"I'm sorry, but I really must be on my way now."

"Okay." She picked him up, still not steadily.

"I can walk you know. In fact, I can walk and talk at the same time." He hoped she would drop him but she didn't until he was brought to the porch. "I still haven't figured out how to talk and chew gum though. Maneuvering words around not only my snaggletooth but also gum is—"

"Bye, bye, kitty." She waved.

"Wait, can you take off this silly dress first?"

"It's a gift to you from me." A kiss was blown, then the door shut.

Pussface's back legs dragged along Idis's wooden floors. The tight dress made half of his body numb. "I need this terrible contraption to be taken off me as soon as possible, otherwise I'll have to go to the vet and have my legs fixed," he grumbled, while sliding into the living room to where the witch sat on her green velvet couch, as usual.

"What's this?" Idis stood in surprise. "Like I said earlier, you aren't taking this job seriously." She glared at the homely cat. "What have you been doing?"

Pussface dragged himself closer to her. "Please, just take it off."

"Hee hee he." She laughed at the sight. "You are literally a drag queen. Get it? Not only are you wearing a dress, which isn't your color by the way, you have to drag yourself around. Hee hee he."

"It's cutting off my circulation. Please!" he begged.

After finally getting it off, the use of his legs slowly came back and Idis became more serious. "Tomorrow you will go through the other half of the neighborhood you didn't get to yet." She sat back down on the couch and pulled a boot off, exposing a gnarly toe poking out through her red sock. "Then there will be no failing in finding Surla. She couldn't have gone far. I need my magic. I am tired of doing everything the hard way." She yanked and yanked at her other boot until finally getting it free. That revealed an even bigger gnarly toe sticking through her socks. "If you fail, *Pusface*, you won't know what hit you!" She threw the boot down hard on the floor for emphasis.

"I know. It's the perfect plan," Pussface heard while balancing on a tree branch, high enough to see the back of a blond girl, talking on the phone through a second story window. "She has changed so much. You would think someone took over her body."

"Someone else taking over her body?" the scroungy cat repeated to himself. "This could be a good clue."

"Yes, she'll get what she deserves." The girl laid back on her bed. "Trying to make me look bad. I know. What a tramp. I bet she thinks every guy in school likes her." She paused. "Well, all the guys do like me." There was another pause, then laughter. "This should teach her to not be so catty."

Catty? Pussface listened. His orange eyes glowed through the window. *Who is this girl she's speaking of?* He was more than curious to know; he needed to know.

"I'm wondering about Chrissy, though," she continued. "You can tell she feels sorry for the nerd. I don't think I should tell her. It will just be you, me, and Lisa that will know… Yeah, she'll probably blab to Cathy."

Cathy! I bet that's the girl's name. Pussface got excited and shifted his weight when suddenly the tree branch was breaking under him.

"Oh no!" he blurted and hugged the branch with all four legs. Right then it snapped, sending him into the bushes. He laid flat on his back, still holding the branch tight and spitting out a leaf.

"Who's there?" the girl's voice called.

Pussface used his last feeling of energy to bolt down the street. He turned, seeing half of the girl's body leaning out the window, the phone still to her ear.

TEN

Surla was clipping the points off of her fake nails in Cathy's bedroom. She decided they were getting in her way. It just wasn't the same having them as a human. Cathy was reading a paperback book on her bed. Her front paws held the pages down. She was on the most suspenseful part of the story.

The sound of the doorknob turning startled them. Cathy's mom caught just a glimpse of the book before Cathy shoved it off the bed. She shook her head, like she imagined it, then said, "Cathy, I'm going to walk to the grocery store. Would you like to come?"

Surla turned to Cathy to see no response. "Um, actually, I think I should clean up my room."

Cat food cans and soda cans were sprawled around the small bedroom. "Okay, I think that's a good idea."

"Okay, bye."

"Bye, honey." The door shut and Cathy dropped to the floor to finish the last page to the chapter she was reading.

This is the perfect place to watch people, Pussface thought as he sat on a bench to the bus stop outside of Revere Park. He was still searching for any suspicious actions which would lead to finding Surla.

Pretty soon a man with an obvious toupee, carrying a briefcase, sat down next to the cat. He was one of the first people Idis had handed the missing cat fliers to. His eyes glanced to Pussface, then turned once more, staring with interest.

"Hey there," the man spoke. "Are you lost? What are you doing here? Hoping to get home this way? First you need some money, little guy. I don't think pets are allowed on board."

Pussface pondered a moment on how funny it would be if he actually decided to respond. *Yeah, maybe if you hide me in your jacket the bus driver won't notice... or I'm just waiting here to pick up some girls, ones with long sexy whiskers and a fluffy tail that will have me running in circles around her all day... or maybe even if I just said 'hi' to the guy he would go crazy; then maybe that carcass, he thinks is hair, will come back to life and will run away.* But Pussface decided to be a nice kitty and not behave that way.

A long blue and white bus came and took the man away to his home, but before he left he stated, "If I had the time, I would take you home right now, but I have a job to go to."

Pussface continued to watch passersby. One with ragged clothes and scraggly hair stopped in front of him. The guy was obviously drunk by his behavior. "H-hey, I know you."

Whatever you say. Pussface didn't take the man seriously.

"Yeah, I-I know you. You're all over the park. Go on home. Be glad you have a home." With those words, the man hopped the stone wall into the park, which in a way was the strange man's home.

More people passing by looked at Pussface with curiosity. *Haven't they ever seen a black cat before?*

Soon a lady holding a grocery bag spotted Pussface also, but she walked over to him, and with a sudden grasp, he was held in her free arm.

Oh no, not again. I don't have time to play another tea party. I'm busy trying to find Surla, the cat muttered in his head.

"Surla? Is that your name?" she said. One of Pussface's ears turned, alert. He wondered how this woman knew that name.

"I guess you are Surla, by the way you responded." She started walking again. "Your owner has been looking for you. The park is packed with your picture."

Pussface looked around, seeing the fliers posted on trees and poles. *If only I was taller, I would have noticed.*

"How about I take you to your home?" She smiled brightly. "But first I'll feed and clean you."

A bath! He imagined himself in the sudsy bubbles. *I hate baths!*

Surla and Cathy heard the front door open and a ruffling of a bag being set down in the kitchen. "Cathy, you'll never guess what I found!" her mother called.

"Probably not," Surla said while coming down the hall to meet her.

"Have you seen those fliers about a missing cat?"

"Yeah." Fear swelled up in her body.

What she found was not what she expected, but was as equally horrifying. Surla silently gasped. *What is he doing here? Idis must have something to do with this!*

Pussface was cradled in Julie's arms. "I just saw fliers everywhere on my way to the grocery store. I bet its owner will be happy that I found her cat. It looks like the streets were brutal to the poor fella."

He always looks that bad, Surla wanted to say.

"What's wrong, Cathy?"

"I think you should take it back home to its owner right now," Surla said almost rudely.

"That's not what you said about Licorice."

"Well, this cat looks like it could have fleas. You don't want Licorice to catch them, do you?" Her eyebrows went up in exclamation.

Pussface looked down at his unhealthy fur. Surla was afraid that her homely cousin would see Cathy if he stayed long. That would definitely reveal her identity for Idis.

"That's why I'm going to give him a flea bath first, then feed him."

"Well you should do it fast before fleas start getting all over the house."

"I agree." She started walking down the hallway toward the bathroom.

Surla ran ahead, entered her room and shut the door before the enemy cat could catch a glimpse of her cat body. Cathy was sitting on the windowsill.

"Cathy," Surla whispered.

She turned around and saw the seriousness in her blue eyes. "What's the matter?" Cathy whispered back.

"Idis is very close to finding us. My cousin is with your mom in the bathroom getting a flea bath." Surla talked faster. "If he sees me, or 'you' I should say, then I don't know what will happen, but it will be bad."

"What should we do? Should I hide somewhere?" Cathy's fur stood up on her back.

"Yeah, that's a good idea. They'll be leaving to take Pussface back home to Idis soon, because she thinks he is me. For now you can hide in…" She looked over the almost bare, neat room.

"How about the closet?" Cathy said.

"All right." Surla slid open a door and Cathy walked in positioning herself behind a stack of shoe boxes. "Don't make any noise."

Pussface had a feeling he was on the right track. He was in the home of a girl named Cathy, whose name he remembered being said the other day by a girl talking on the phone. That girl had mentioned how much Cathy had changed. Also, Cathy was acting very strange when he just saw her.

Cathy's mom was stretching some yellow gloves over her hands. She poured in the flea bath and ran warm water. This was the moment Pussface would have to endure. He liked his fleas. They were a part of him. In a way, he enjoyed scratching and feeling dirty. In a moment, that freedom would be gone. In fact, he hadn't had a bath in such a long time, he forgot how it felt.

"Okay, Surla. Come on." He was lifted off the toilet. Pussface wriggled around, fighting the hold, but stopped suddenly, knowing from experience, it was not worth the fight. Humans are much stronger than cats. He would just have to face his fear: cleanliness.

"Gosh, with the name Surla, you would think you were a girl, wouldn't you?" She scrubbed his fur around his neck. Muck, dirt, and dandruff was turning the water brown. It felt as if he had lost some weight. *I am actually feeling better*, he thought.

"You are really dirty." She refilled the sink. "You aren't anything like the cat we found a while ago, except for the black fur." She had just let the cat out of the bag, figuratively speaking. Now Pussface was almost positive Surla was living in the house.

She probably was in that girl Cathy's body. His fur was the shiniest he had ever seen it. The nice lady began to dry him off with a towel. *If only there was a way I could stay here longer so I could see the cat this lady told me about. Then I would know without a doubt.*

"Where are my keys?" Cathy's mom frantically looked all over the kitchen. What she didn't know was that Pussface had dragged them onto the floor into the living room, to have more time to finish thinking over his strategy of staying longer.

He sat on the coffee table near the keys. His orange eyes stared at the flier of Surla in thought. *Aha!* He came to a solution. Grabbing the pen that sat next to it with both paws, he attempted to get the cap off. Finally after chewing it to bits, it came loose. Slowly, he changed the address on the paper from 713 Shadyside Street to 718.

ELEVEN

"Are you sure this isn't your cat?" Cathy's mom held Pussface in her arms. His fur looked healthier and a red bow was tied around his neck.

The elderly lady looked at the cat, then back at her. "What did you say?" She cupped her ear that had the hearing aid.

"Are you sure this isn't your cat?" she said again, this time raising her voice.

Pussface looked down at the porch and watched Diamond, the fluffy white cat. She sat licking her fur like usual. He then shifted his body to see Idis's old house across the street.

"Yes, I am sure. He is not my cat. My cat's name is Diamond. I have had her for seven years." The door was then shut.

"Well, I'm sorry, Surla." She rubbed Pussface under the chin. "The flier says 718 Shadyside Street. Maybe your owner is not only deaf but is going blind, too."

They descended the steps and went to her car. Pussface looked back at the lady's cat. When Diamond finally made eye contact, he winked.

"We can't keep this cat. We have to find it a home," Surla argued.

"I agree, but I am not going out again today. He'll just have to stay here for now." Julie and Pussface sat on the couch, while Surla stood across from them with her arms folded. "Go get Licorice. I want to see how they react to one another."

"But, she is sleeping." Surla really didn't know if she was sleeping or not.

"Go wake her up then."

Surla reluctantly obeyed. The two cats met eye-to-eye. Pussface finally knew he was right—Surla was living there.

Monday, at school, the only thing Surla could think about was Pussface. She couldn't trust him at all. They had been cousins for centuries. She knew him too well. In fact, she feared that right at that moment, as she sat in Chemistry, Pussface could escape to go tell Idis where to find her.

"Cathy," she heard a distant whisper becoming louder. "Cathy…" Someone touched her shoulder. Surla turned to see Todd. No one else was in the room except for them and the teacher, Mrs. Fitzgerald. "The bell rang."

"Oh, I'm sorry. I'm really out of it today." Surla grabbed her backpack quickly and smiled dumbly.

As they walked out into the hallway, a whiff of Todd's cologne drifted to Surla's nostrils. She had smelled the cool scent all day and enjoyed it very much. A couple times she felt like putting her nose right up to his neck and breathing in deeply.

"You still grounded?" he asked.

"Yeah."

"That's too bad." He looked very sincere.

"Yeah," she said again.

"When do you get off of groundation?"

"Possibly by Friday."

"That would be perfect! I'm playing against our rival school, Jefferson High. Maybe you can come watch me."

"Maybe." Surla's mouth widened into a smile.

"So, why didn't you escape and tell Idis when you had the chance?" Surla asked, surprised to see Pussface sitting on the bed next to Cathy.

"I still can." His skinny body stretched across the covers. "I just figured I would stay a while longer and enjoy the luxuries of this place."

"All day he has been drinking up my milk and napping on my bed," Cathy whined. "And he sheds more than any cat I have ever known." She blew on Pussface, causing fur to fly. "See what I mean?"

"How long are you planning on staying?" Surla secretly hoped it would be long enough to postpone the witch from discovering her hideout.

"Well, I might leave in a couple days or I might leave tomorrow," he said nonchalantly on purpose, "...or maybe I could go early in the morning before you wake up. I don't want Idis to get too upset. You know how she is, Surla. If I don't go back soon, I could get one of her boots thrown to my head."

"You dirty hairball! Poor excuse for a cat! You are saying that to make me mad." Surla stuck her face right in front of his. "Remember, Pusface, for the time being, I am bigger than you. Idis can go stuff both her boots right in her mouth, because I don't give a rat's tail about her. You are going to stay here as long as I want."

Pussface extended sharp nails on his right paw. "I think I have a right to leave when I want."

Surla stepped back, but not from fear. "That's how I felt the day I ran away from Idis."

Pussface's claws retracted. Just then the phone rang. Surla stared at him as she went to answer it from off of Cathy's bedside dresser. "Hello?" Surla's tone changed to sweet.

"Hey, Cathy. What's up?" she heard the male voice say.

"I'm sorry, who is this?"

"How many other guys have your number?" he joked. "This is Craig."

"Oh, Craig," she repeated for Cathy to hear.

"Craig?!" Cathy jumped up excitedly. Her tail stood like a candy cane.

"Watch out." Pussface was making fun. "You'll jump right out of your fur. Who is this Craig guy anyway?" No one answered him.

"I figured I would give you a call," Craig continued. "Are you busy?"

"What kind of busy?"

"Too busy to go out and do something with me?"

Cathy is getting asked out on a date! "No I'm not busy," Surla responded coolly.

"Good... do you wanna grab a milkshake with me? I can pick you up in a half hour."

"Sure, that would be..." She suddenly remembered Cathy's mother getting mad at her, punishing her for a week for catching a boy in the house. "Wait. I'm sorry, Craig... I can't. Tonight is bad. My mom grounded me."

"Oh... Okay." There was a pause. "What about this Friday? Are you free then?"

"I'm pretty sure."

"All right then. Don't get into anymore trouble." He laughed.

"I won't, Craig." She knew it was coming to the end of their conversation.

"See you at school. I'm playing basketball against you tomorrow in P.E." He sounded ready for more competition.

"I know. I've been practicing my skills in the backyard," Surla kidded.

"I'm ready. See you tomorrow."

"Okay. Bye."

Surla hung up, then plopped on the bed next to Cathy. "Didn't I tell you I would hook him by my cat-like ways?"

"Did he just ask me on a date?!"

"Yep, but it would be even better if you could go yourself."

"That's okay. I'm on a roll having you be me."

Pussface's tongue curled into an exaggerated yawn. "Lonely souls are lonely because they don't have enough guts to go out and do things themselves. They don't interact well. They have poor social skills."

"What is he talking about?" Cathy asked.

Surla knew he was speaking of the Black Cats' Curse. Surla didn't want Cathy to know that part—the part where it only works with lonely souls. "Pussface likes to ramble a lot. He doesn't make any sense most of the time." She shot him a mad look for him to stay quiet. She knew it would be a sensitive subject for Cathy to hear.

It was getting late out. Surla was tired and needed her sleep for school the next day. Cathy was overjoyed from Craig's call and soon was dreaming about being human again and kissing him. Surla made sure Pussface slept on the rug. There wasn't enough room for the three of them to be on the bed, and even if there was room, she wouldn't have it any other way. The window next to her was locked tight to be sure the obnoxious cat couldn't escape.

The next morning, Cathy's clock radio turned on as an alarm to wake Surla. It was 6:30. She blinked a few times and felt a chilly breeze cross her arms as she still laid at the bottom of the bed. Surla glanced around to find the cold source. The window! It was open! *But I made sure it was locked!* she remembered. Surla looked for Pussface. She searched around every corner of the bedroom. He wasn't found. Finally she looked under the bed and woke up Cathy in the process by frantically throwing the covers back and forth.

"What's wrong?" Cathy asked, alarmed.

"He's gone. Pussface is gone!"

TWELVE

Pussface had snuck out and Surla felt there was a slim chance that he wouldn't tell Idis. *I should have tied him to the bed-post!* Surla thought while leaving for school.

As the next few days slowly passed, the scare caused by Idis finding out decreased. It was now Friday and Surla's more ordinary thoughts were taking over.

Since they played a new sport for P.E., basketball, the teams switched around. So, they couldn't go up against Craig and Travis anymore. Surla and Chrissy now played against Olly Renfro and Dave Healy. They both were wimpy and couldn't make one basket. They tripped over each other so much, defense was almost not needed at all.

"It's been an easy week, hasn't it?" Chrissy said while changing out of her gym clothes.

"Yeah, it has," Surla said, after putting a tight red shirt over head. She noticed how upbeat Chrissy's attitude had been since they changed sports from tennis to basketball.

"What are you doing tonight?" Chrissy tied her shoelaces on a locker room bench.

"I think I might be doing something with Craig."

"What?" she said, disapprovingly. "But tonight there is a really important football game for our school. We're competing against Jefferson High. How can you miss that?"

"You like football?" Surla was surprised.

"Well, if it has to do with our school. I have a lot of spirit, you know."

"Oh yeah, Todd plays tonight, doesn't he?" Surla recalled him asking her to come and watch him play.

"Yes he does. Come on. You should go." Chrissy was persistent.

"What, go with you?"

"Well, no. But just go. It will be fun."

"Why does it matter? The only reason I would go is to support Todd. Besides I have a date with Craig tonight." Surla finished dressing and walked to a nearby mirror to check out how her eye makeup was doing.

"I think Todd likes you," Chrissy said, while stuffing her dirty clothes into a gym bag.

"Huh?" Surla instantly turned to her. She often wondered if Todd liked Cathy, but wasn't sure. *How could someone be so sure? Was it that obvious to others?* "Why do you say that?"

"Cathy, it's only obvious. He's always around you, sitting next to you, helping you with your work in the library. I mean, it's not every day that you see the quarterback helping someone with their studies in the *library*. Yes, I could just see you two together right now. A perfect couple."

Could she just be saying this because she doesn't want Cathy to be with Craig? She kept warning me not to get with him. Or does Todd really like Cathy? "What about Craig?"

"What about him?" she said as if he were her bratty brother. "Craig has a super ego."

That was the end of their conversation. Surla left for her next class, Chemistry. Everywhere she turned she saw Halloween decorations. Never had she seen so much of the color orange. That reminded Surla of the party that was to be taking place at Revere Park.

"Hey, you earned a B+ on your test," Todd said as he leaned, looking over Surla's Chemistry paper.

"Yep, thanks to you." She smiled. Surla had been concentrating on Todd's actions, because of what Chrissy said about him liking Cathy. She wondered about each little thing he did. Was it flirting or not flirting? And would it be noticeable to others? *When he leaned over, his shoulder touched mine; is this a sign he likes me and wants to be close? Oh, maybe I'm being too analytical.*

"As a thanks, how about you come to the game tonight and root for your number one football player?" He smiled.

Is that any normal smile? Would he smile so sweetly to any girl? What about how he said my number one football player? It sounded a little flirtatious.

"Well, Cath? Are you going to go?"

"Sure," she answered absentmindedly.

"Hurry up!" Cathy jumped onto the bathroom counter, looking at Surla curl her eyelashes in the magnified mirror. "Craig will be here soon."

"Shhh!" She waved her free hand at Cathy. "Your mom will hear you."

"Sorry, it's just that I'm so nervous. It's my first date, with the hottest guy at school."

"Don't worry about it." Surla placed the curler back into a floral makeup bag and proceeded with some shimmery eyeshadow. "I'll be ready on time."

"I hope so." Cathy took a deep breath to calm herself. She then stared at her human profile. Surla was whisking and applying makeup like she had been practicing her whole life. She stared at the dramatic improvement that was appearing before her eyes. Her features were standing out so natural and pretty, from her rosy lips to her cleanly plucked eyebrows. For just a moment, Cathy believed she looked better than Tiffany.

"Cathy, we can't do this for much longer."

"Do what?"

"Stay switched. I think just for another week will be good enough. We can switch back on Halloween night. That way, Idis will be at The Annual Witches' Ball and we can recover the Spellbook safely. Also I would have gotten Craig by then to be wrapped around your finger in time for you two to go to the Halloween Party together at Revere Park." Surla zipped the makeup bag and went to Cathy's room to finish off her wardrobe.

"Just one more week?" Cathy followed her in on little paws. "That seems so soon."

"Cathy, it's the best time. Do you want to stay a cat forever?" Surla picked out a pair of white shoes to go with the nice khaki pants and white, silk shirt.

"No. I guess that is the best time, but what if Pussface tells Idis before then?"

"I don't know. We just have to think positive. Idis hasn't come for us yet. Maybe Pussface didn't tell her for some reason."

Cathy leaped over to the windowsill and stared outside. Surla ran her fingers through her hair that was let down for the occasion. Soon headlights were spotted coming down the road from a distance. Cathy's eyes followed them intensely until the car pulled up into the driveway. It was the red sports car. "He's here! He's here! He's here!" Cathy whispered in excitement.

"Okay, okay." Surla stood straight. "How do I look?"

"Cathy, I think your date is here!" Julie yelled, followed by the sound of the doorbell.

"Thank you!" Surla called.

"You look great!" Cathy said.

"You mean *you* look great." Surla fingered her hair once more before walking to the living room. Cathy followed closely behind.

Craig wore a red polo shirt and black jeans. His hair was the same as usual, brushed with no gel, his bangs split down the middle hanging passed his eyes.

"Hey!" he said, noticing Surla. His car keys jingled in his right hand. "You look nice."

"I was thinking the same about you."

"I expect you'll be back by eleven," Julie told Surla.

"Mother." Surla acted embarrassed. "What about eleven-thirty?"

"Well, all right. I guess another half hour does no harm." She smiled at the two. "I expected him to be that guy who was over the other day."

"No, Mom. I told you already, Todd was just helping me study." That reminded Surla once again about the football game. Guilt entered her mind since she accidentally told Todd she would go.

"Okay, we better be on our way then." Craig opened the door.

"You two have fun!" Mom called out, as they walked to his car. She stood watching until the engine started, then waved good-bye before closing the door.

As they drove out of the driveway, Surla said, "You know, I never did ask you where we were going tonight."

"I thought I would make it a surprise."

"Can I have a clue?"

"It will be a place where we can get to know each other a lot better."

"I guess it's not a movie." She laughed, expecting him to also, but he didn't. "You know, because you can't talk much during a movie."

"I know." He smiled, turning down a different road. Each road he drove down seemed more secluded than the last. After a while, they were heading down a long dirt path through the woods.

"How will you know your way back?" Surla became worried.

"I won't get lost." He was very confident.

Surla saw tire marks in the dirt already, and the car soon stopped in front of a lake. The moon was casting a white glow across the soft ripples of water. *How romantic*, Surla thought. Craig took off his seat belt and turned to look at Surla while removing her seat belt.

"Here we are." His eyes appeared as a darker blue.

"It's beautiful," she said while still looking at him.

"Just like you." He brushed a hand softly across her cheek and through her hair. "It's amazing how I never noticed you before."

"Yeah, well, I noticed you." Surla thought about kissing him that instant. *Go ahead! Kiss him! Kiss him! Kiss him!* she repeated in her head. So slowly, with passion, she leaned in, opened her lips, and licked his cheek.

"That's different." Craig liked that. He leaned over to her and kissed her on the mouth, his tongue touching hers in a french kiss. *Now that's different.* Surla was enjoying it very much. They did that for a long while when suddenly he pulled back to open his door. Surla noticed the windows were all fogged up.

She saw his chest rise in a deep breath. "Let's go out to the lake."

"Okay." Surla was becoming fond of Craig. After all, she was in a body with human hormones. But she knew it was was more of a duty rather than for pleasure.

Craig held her hand as they walked to the water. It was even more beautiful to see it up close, and the sound of crickets chirping was nature's way of setting an even more romantic mood.

Craig started to take off his shoes.

"What are you doing?"

"Let's go for a dip." His socks were taken off.

"Go swimming?"

"Yeah, come on. It's a warm night."

Cats do not like to go in water, let alone swim. She looked above to see dark clouds floating by. "What if it rains?"

"That will make it even more fun." He pulled his polo shirt off. His chest and abs were defined nicely. "I'm a water polo player. I'm used to it anyway. Come on, start taking off your clothes."

"Take off my clothes?"

"Yeah, you don't want that silk shirt to get ruined, do you?"

"Well, no."

"Then come on. Haven't you ever gone skinny-dipping before?" He laughed.

"Skinny-dipping?" Surla had never even heard of it before.

"I guess not." He smiled, looking her up and down. "It's all right. You haven't done much with anyone, I can tell. If you want, keep your underwear on."

Surla hesitated while watching him unbelt and pull off his jeans.

"Okay." She gave into his calling and took off her white tennis shoes, then her pants, and lastly her blouse, which she folded on top of her other clothes, so as not to get ruined.

They both left on their underwear. As Craig entered the lake, his boxer shorts filled with water, making them look like a floating device. Surla felt embarrassed she wore a bra and panty-set with little puppy dogs on them; not because it was childish, but just for the fact that they were puppy dogs. The water was surprisingly a mild temperature.

"Come over to me." Craig was further out and motioned her with a finger.

Surla had never gone swimming before and was fearful to learn. "Craig, I can't really swim," she admitted.

"Can't swim?" He looked very surprised. "Well, okay. We'll just stay over here." He swam closer to her. They were up to their chests in water. "Cute undies." He smiled, looking at her puppy bra.

"I know. I hate it, too." She laughed.

At the same time Surla and Craig were at the lake, Washington High was playing football against their rival school. It was a few minutes into half-time and Chrissy was returning to the bleachers, carrying snacks. Tiffany and Lisa sat with a plaid blanket across their laps.

"Here's our dinner." She could hardly hold the three hot dogs and soft drinks. Lisa helped by grabbing her and Tiffany's portions.

"Oh, Chrissy, I didn't want a hot dog." Tiffany looked around, then whispered, "You know I'm on a diet."

"Oops. I'm sorry. I forgot." She sat down next to her. "I guess I can save it for my brother when I get home."

"You do that." The hot dog was handed back.

Chrissy set it on the cold iron bench. "Hey, guys, do you think I can have some of that blanket, too? It's pretty chilly out here."

Lisa sighed and Tiffany spoke, "I don't think it's long enough." Chrissy saw it falling onto the seat in front of them, but decided to say nothing. She was getting more bored as time went on.

Chrissy had lied to Surla. She really didn't care about football. It was just a way to try and get Cathy away from Craig. Chrissy was afraid for her. She knew how jealous Tiffany could get. The marching band in the middle of the field was also annoying her. All the drumming over and over was droning on her mind. Soon she was in a daydream. Her wide brown eyes stared ahead as she took the last bite of her hot dog.

"Hey, girls," she heard a guy call, breaking her gaze. It was Todd, re-energized from half-time. Being the star quarterback took a lot of sweat and Chrissy could see it across his forehead. His helmet dangled in his right hand.

"Oh, hi, Todd!" Tiffany smiled. "How ya doin'? You looked really good out there and because of *you* we're winning."

83

"Yeah, it's been a good game so far," he said, looking at all the people around them. Chrissy could tell he wasn't in the mood for chit chat. He was looking for someone. "But, uh, I just came over to ask if any of you have seen Cathy around."

"Oh." Tiffany's smile faded, then reappeared suddenly. "Oh, yes. I-I did see her a while ago."

"You did?" He paid full attention to her now. "Where?"

Lisa looked at her friend curiously.

"Yeah," she continued, "I saw Cathy during the first quarter." One eyebrow raised. "Some really hot looking guy came and sat next to her. They were talking the whole time. I bet she didn't pay attention to any of the plays out on the field, 'cause they started their own action, right behind us."

Todd looked stunned. "Really?!"

"Yep, and soon after the second quarter began, they left together... hand-in-hand."

Chrissy's mouth dropped as she turned her head away from the conversation. She knew Tiffany was lying and Todd was believing every word of it.

"Well." He turned his head also, then looked back. "Thanks for telling me." Then the red helmet was placed back on his head and he went back toward the field.

"You're welcome!" Tiffany yelled.

The majorettes started the last performance before the third quarter, twirling their batons in perfect timing and order.

"I can't believe you told him that." Chrissy shook her head, but her friends just turned to each other and laughed.

"If only he knew where she really was, huh, Lisa," Tiffany said.

"Yes. You are sooo bad." Lisa laughed more.

"Where? Where's Cathy?" Chrissy asked.

"Nowhere." Tiffany ignored her.

"Yeah... in the middle of nowhere," Lisa said.

"What do you mean?" Chrissy was becoming very worried. She knew they were keeping something awful from her. "Where's Cathy?"

"Don't say anything to her," Tiffany warned Lisa.

"Oh, what's the big deal? It probably already happened."

"What?" Chrissy pleaded to know.

"Cathy got abandoned on her date with Craig, with no way to get home, except to walk most of the way." Lisa laughed as if it were a really funny joke. "Left at a lake."

"Shut up, Lisa!" Tiffany slapped the girl's arm.

"And you two were behind this?"

"Yep." Lisa ignored Tiffany's demand. "Well, mostly Tiff was."

"That's sick... really sick." Chrissy scooted over a bit. "Look at the weather. There's rain clouds. What will she do? She could catch pneumonia and the nearest lake is miles from here."

"Oh, settle down, Chrissy." Tiffany took hold of her shoulder. "I always thought you were too much of a 'goody-goody.' Only my mom would have been worrying about something like pneumonia."

"Really?" Chrissy put on a fake smile and reached for her soda. "Would a 'goody-goody' do this?" Orange soda was poured onto the girls' blanket, immediately soaking to their laps as Chrissy stood up. "I guess there *isn't* any room for me." She walked off quickly, not caring to see their response.

"I can't believe she did that!" she heard Tiffany say, exasperated.

Chrissy jogged over to Todd, who was stretching on the sidelines. "Todd, I need to tell you something."

He lunged forward, stretching his calves. "What is it?"

"It's about Cathy."

"Cathy?" He looked up with more interest. "What is it? I have to go play soon."

The majorettes were going into their last routine and Chrissy had to hurry up. "Okay." She brushed her hair behind her ears. "I was sitting with Tiffany and Lisa as you saw earlier, and the truth is Cathy didn't leave with some cute guy. She didn't come at all because..."

"Yeah, hurry please." Todd fixed his knee pads.

"Because Craig took her on a date and…"

"Okay, that's enough I wanna hear." He turned away and started walking out on the field with his teammates.

"He left her there, Todd! At a lake, with no way home… as a mean joke!" She called out while the band was drumming to pump up the crowd.

"What?!" He turned quickly, with concern in his eyes.

"Yeah! Meet me at the refreshment stand after the game!"

He nodded and went to his position. Chrissy watched the rest of the game from the opposing school's side, to be as far away from Tiffany and Lisa as possible. She was sure they saw her talking to Todd.

For the rest of the night, Washington High didn't score. Todd was obviously distracted thinking about Cathy. His throws were constantly off, and what made it even worse was whenever the team messed up, Chrissy had to hear everyone around her cheer in excitement.

At the lake, Surla was wondering if she and Craig were getting too intimate. They had been kissing for a very long time now. *What would Cathy think? Would she be happy or mad to know what I was doing right now?* But she went along with it still. His hands rubbed up and down her back. It was all okay with her until she felt his fingers working the back of her bra to come off.

"Stop," Surla said, pulling back.

"What's the matter?"

"You said I didn't have to take off any more."

"You don't have to…" He smiled. "I'll take it off for you."

"What?" She was surprised he would say something like that.

"I said, I'll take it off for you. You don't have to do it."

"Get away from me." Surla took a couple steps backward, feeling the mushy floor of the lake squish between her toes.

"You aren't as mature as I thought you would be." He walked toward her.

"I said, get away."

"Cathy." He reached for her arm.

"Get away!" Surla pushed him off of her, but in the process made herself go back further. The water encircled her neck.

"Fine." He put up his arms, in a surrendering stance. He then quickly swam to shore, grabbed his clothes, and headed to his car. "I thought you were different than before, Cathy! I wasn't going to follow through with this, but all you are is a tease!" He turned the key and the ignition started.

"Wait!" Surla knew she had no other way home. "Don't leave! Wait!" But it was too late. Craig sped, like usual, leaving only a cloud of dust.

"Now what can I do?" She felt short of breath. The first thing she had to do was reach the beach. She was at least thankful she hadn't stepped back any further.

Slowly, she walked back toward shore, but not before heavy drops were hitting her face. It began raining, like she thought it would, and her body shivered. The drops fell harder and harder, stinging her skin. Her hair matted to her face and neck. When Surla noticed all that was left of her clothes were Cathy's shoes, she started to cry. Craig was even more rotten than she thought.

"Poor Cathy," she cried. "I-I shouldn't h-have been so stupid!" She wiped her face with her forearm, even though the tears blended with the rain.

After the football game ended, Todd and Chrissy met up at the refreshment stand as agreed.

"Did I hear you correctly?" He took off his helmet and brushed a hand through his hair.

"Yes. Cathy is stuck miles away from here at a lake with no way home." Just then the rain started to pour. "Oh no, what should we do?"

"Did you drive here?"

"No. I just live a couple of blocks away."

"Okay, good. How about you ride along with me, while we look for this place? My cell is in the car in case we need to call someone for help."

The rain made Chrissy's mascara run. "Okay, sounds good. Let's hurry."

Surla hiked through the woods with underwear and shoes as her only covering. Her arms were folded tightly as she consistently trembled. Cathy's once sparkling blue eyes now looked vacant like a zombie. Surla had stopped crying; sadness was replaced by anger.

It seemed as if she had been trudging through mud for miles before she came upon a phone. It was in a booth of an empty parking lot. Cathy had taught Surla every trick there was about phones the day Craig asked for her phone number.

Her fingers were jittery as she started dialing a collect call, but hung up before finishing. "If I call her mom to pick me up in the middle of nowhere in my underwear because my date abandoned me, that would make her not trust Cathy's wisdom." She could dial 911, but even to have an officer see her tricked like that felt too humiliating. Surla contemplated a long time before she thought of someone who she could trust and confide in to help.

It was extremely dark out and the rain made it worse as it slammed against Todd's windshield. "Craig is a jerk. I could've told Cathy he was bad news." He gripped the steering wheel like it was Craig's neck.

Chrissy nodded as she helped read road signs. They were headed to Lake Sequoia. "I tried to warn her also. I knew Tiffany was capable of doing something like this. I feel really stupid. I remember when Cathy asked me why I was friends with Tiffany."

"What did you tell her?"

Chrissy laughed at the foolish comment that was going to come out of her mouth. "I told her because I played Barbie with her when I was just four. I've put up with her for a long time."

"People change," was his response.

"Yeah, I know. Like Cathy. She made an incredible change."

"For the better." A smile crept on Todd's face. "The truth is, though, I always thought Cathy was pretty and nice, but when she came to school a couple weeks ago looking, you know, so different, all I could think was, Wow! She also talks a lot more."

"That's cute, Todd." Chrissy leaned her head on the door's cold window. They were nearing Lake Sequoia. The speedometer got higher in anticipation, when suddenly Todd's cell phone rang. Chrissy's nerves jumped.

"Hello?" Todd answered.

"Todd?" he heard the faint voice say.

"Yeah, is this Cathy?"

"Yes!" She laughed, happy to have reached him. Surla almost forgot his number. One day while writing notes back and forth in Chemistry class, she slid the folded paper in her lap and opened it so no one could see. It surprised her to find 555-7327 written down. "How did the game go?"

"We lost," he said quickly. "Where are you, Cathy? I'm here with Chrissy, looking for you. We know what happened."

Surla's voice choked up. "You know? How?"

"Don't cry. We're coming to get you. Where are you calling from?"

"I-I'm at a vacant gas station, using the payphone. I think it's at the first station off the exit, by the lake."

"Okay, we're not far from there. Do you want to stay on the line with me?"

"Actually, I think I should go. I don't want anyone to see me. It's kind of an embarrassing situation. I'll be hiding behind a bush. You could just honk your horn three times so I know it's you."

"Okay, Cath. Stay safe. I'll be right there."

"Thanks, Todd."

The blue truck soon pulled up to a small gas station. The parking lot was empty and boards were nailed up in the windows. A sign said, Temporarily CLOSED For Reconstruction.

Honk! Honk! Honk! That was Surla's signal, he was there. Chrissy and Todd peered out the rain-splattered windows impatiently. Thunder boomed and lightning that looked like spider webs flashed through the sky.

"Where is she?" Chrissy's brown eyes searched desperately.

"There's the only bush I can see." Todd pointed to a hedge fifteen feet away from a phone-booth.

"Are we at the wrong place?" Chrissy asked, worried.

"I don't know. I mean, I don't think so… Maybe I should honk again." Honk! Honk! Honk! Another ten seconds passed.

"Where is she?" Todd was tense. "Okay, I'm going to look." He opened his door. Instantly, sheets of rain poured in and onto the seat. Thunder boomed again, then more lightning.

"Hurry back, Todd! This is scary." Chrissy said a quick prayer. She saw his shadowed figure run to the hedge. He carefully looked behind it, then dropped to the ground suddenly.

Todd was horrified by what he saw: Cathy face down in the mud. Her cotton underwear clung to her wet body. "Cathy! Oh, God, please don't let this be what I'm thinking." He lifted her head and listened for breath. He was happy to feel the cool exhalation on his cheek. He turned her over, sliding one arm through the mud and under her back. His other arm held under her knees, so he could cradle her in his arms. Slowly, he lifted her limp body, then jogged to the truck.

"Open the door!" he called to Chrissy.

Chrissy obeyed immediately. Her hands shook tremendously as she helped drag Surla inside. Todd shut the door and the fainted sixteen-year-old's body laid across their laps.

"Is she alive?" Chrissy asked.

"Yes. She's still breathing. She must have fainted, walking so far in this weather. Cathy!" he said, trying to wake her from the deep state.

"Cathy!" they both said over and over. Chrissy held and rubbed her icy hands. Todd turned on the heater, then proceeded by shaking her shoulders.

"She needs something warm. Why is she in her underwear?" Chrissy said, then instantly pulled off her own sweater-jacket to place over Surla.

Color was coming back to her cheeks and lips. Her wet eyelashes fluttered and the first vision she saw was Todd's green eyes staring down with delight. "She's awake!" Surla heard him say.

"Oh, good!" Chrissy exhaled in relief.

"Meow?" Surla uttered.

"Did she just say 'meow'?" Todd asked.

"She must be delirious."

"Wh-what just happened?" Surla sat up dizzily.

"You fainted, but you're all right now," Chrissy said.

"Craig and Tiffany need the daylights knocked out of them for doing this to you," Todd said, heated.

"Why Tiffany?" Surla asked.

"She was behind the whole idea of leaving you there," Chrissy revealed to her. "I found out at the football game. That's why Todd and I came as quick as we could."

"Boy, did I mess up." Surla held Chrissy's sweater tightly.

"It's not your fault," Todd said.

Surla saw the digital clock above the radio said 11:25. "Oh no! I'm supposed to be home in five minutes."

"It took us a half hour to get here." Todd pulled out of the parking lot, heading back down the highway. "You'll never make it in time. Maybe we should take you to the hospital. You don't look so good."

"Thanks, but really I'm feeling better!"

"Hey, I have an idea," Chrissy said. "Tiffany was going to spend the night at my house tonight, but no way is it going to happen after what she did to you. Do you wanna come over instead? It will be a good way for your mom to not worry about you."

"Yeah, that does sound smart." Surla smiled.

"Here, you can use my cell phone." Todd handed it to her.

The rain was still coming down hard.

"Mom?" Surla said after reaching an answer on the other end.

"Yes, Cathy. You're supposed to be here any minute. What's going on?"

"Well, um, after the school's football game, I ran into my friend Chrissy and, well, I was wondering if I could maybe spend the night at her house tonight."

There was a sigh. "Well, I don't know. Is it all right with her parents?"

"Yes. I know for sure."

"I guess it's okay then, but I was really interested to hear how your date went."

The horrible night's incident flashed through Surla's mind again. "I don't think there will be a second date."

"Oh, I'm sorry to hear that. At least you went and gave it a shot. Have fun with your new friend Chrissy. I'm glad you're being more social lately, honey."

Surla just smiled, then Cathy's mom continued, "Be home around noon tomorrow."

"Okay, thanks, Mom. Bye."

Surla hung up and returned the phone to Todd.

"Cathy, there's some sweats in the backseat you can put on. I'm sure you must be freezing." Todd pointed to the red pile.

"Thanks." Surla quickly put them on and maneuvered her wet bra off without anyone seeing.

"Um, Cathy…" Chrissy turned in her seat. "Do you mind me asking what happened to your clothes?"

Surla laughed. "No, I don't mind. I know this situation looks really bad, but it's probably not what you're thinking."

Todd was especially interested in what the explanation would be.

"Well, I went swimming in the lake with Craig. He talked me into taking off my clothes, since I was wearing a silk shirt. I've seen less in bathing suits, so I didn't think much about it, but when he tried to go further than that I wouldn't let him. That's when he sped off with my clothes. I should have scratched him or bit his ear like I wanted."

"Oh, I'll do more than that to him when I see him," Todd said, angered. "I hope you don't think all guys are like that."

"No, I don't think all guys are jerks. Especially not you! Tonight you saved me, Todd, and so did you, Chrissy. You two are like my heroes."

"What do you say about your 'heroes' wanting to take you out to eat?" Todd looked at Chrissy and she agreeably smiled.

"That is an offer I cannot refuse." Surla was feeling warm again and her spirits were lifting, but her stomach growled of hunger. "It has to be a place with chicken though. I love to eat birds."

"Oh yeah, and I love burgers, so let's go eat some cow and birds," Todd quipped.

THIRTEEN

The three sat at a booth next to a window. They were lucky to have such nice seating, since Rita's Grill was a popular diner. There was always conversation and laughter twenty-four hours a day. Surla ordered a chicken sandwich, Chrissy ordered a soup and salad, and Todd sat across the table, chomping down a burger with fries. After a half hour passed, the food was eaten off their plates, with much help from Todd, and conversation was dying down.

"Well, Cathy, are you feeling better?" Todd asked.

"Yes, I am." Surla stretched her arms over her head and leaned back. In doing that, she caught a glimpse of someone outside resembling Craig. She looked again and sure enough it was Craig—entering his red sports car with Tiffany! "He's here!" Surla blurted out.

"Who is? Craig?" Todd and Chrissy said in unison. They looked out the window into the rainy parking lot.

"Yes! He just got in his car with Tiffany."

"That's him all right." Chrissy knew from all the rides home.

"I'm gonna have a talk with him," Todd said threateningly.

They instantly rushed toward the door.

"Wait!" a woman's voice called from behind. They turned to see the heavy-set waitress who served them. "You aren't leaving without paying."

Craig's headlights were seen leaving down the highway. "Man!" Todd said loud enough for some people to stop eating to see what the problem was. Disappointed, he walked to the register with Chrissy and Surla. "What's the bill?"

The waitress ripped the receipt loose. "It comes out to nineteen dollars and sixty four cents."

Todd pulled his wallet from his back pocket, paid, and took three chocolate mints before leaving.

The rain slowed to a soft pitter-patter when they drove away from Rita's Grill. Surla fell asleep easily; her head, at first leaning back, found its way to Todd's shoulder. Chrissy was wide awake, staring ahead. There was a car stopped at the side of the road, down the way a bit. Chrissy turned around in her seat to look at it. "Hey, Todd, that was Craig's car back there."

"What?" He slowed down. "I think you're right." He did a U-turn on the slippery road. His truck stopped in front of the red sports car. They let Surla sleep, so she could rejuvenate, while Todd went to settle the situation.

Todd ran his hands through his dark, wet hair before approaching the driver's side window. He knocked on it, then Craig rolled it down.

"Hey, Todd. I'm having some car trouble. I was coming home with Tiffany and it just stalled."

The blonde leaned forward and smiled. Her lipstick was smeared across her cheek. "Do you think you can call someone for help?"

"Call for help? Yeah right. Why don't I just leave the two of you stranded like you did to Cathy?" His eyebrows furrowed.

Craig turned to Tiffany. "Um, Craig, I think Chrissy might've told him."

"What?! I thought Chrissy wasn't gonna know about it." He then turned to Todd again. "Listen, man, it's not like it sounds. You should've seen the way Cathy was acting."

Todd gripped the collar to Craig's polo shirt. "I think we better take this outside." His muscles dragged Craig through the open window and onto the wet concrete.

"What the heck is your problem?!" Craig stood, looking down at his ripped shirt.

"You're my problem and I think it needs solving quickly." He punched him in the face, causing his nose to bleed. "That's for Cathy."

Craig shook his head and felt the blood. Then, like a dry twig, his anger snapped. He punched at Todd, but most throws were dodged.

Todd punched him back in the stomach. "Say you're scum. Say it!"

Craig was getting weaker. His body hunched over, but still no words came out of his mouth. Todd pinned him against the hood. "Say it!"

"No," came the choked response.

Todd punched him once more. Craig's blood stained his white T-shirt.

"Stop!" Tiffany yelled. "You're really hurting him!"

"Okay, I'm stopping." Todd clenched his fists in retreat.

Craig moaned in pain.

Cathy was still sleeping deeply when Chrissy exited the truck. She walked to the passenger side of the car and opened the door. Tiffany's eyes were wide with surprise as she scooted over to the driver's seat. "I'm just taking Cathy's clothes back," Chrissy said and reached to the back seat where she saw the silk shirt and khaki pants.

Chrissy protected the shirt from the rain by sticking it under her own as she ran back to the truck and tossed it inside.

Todd was still busy arguing with Craig when she returned to Tiffany. The car door was still open. Chrissy smiled and reached to the ground. With a light laugh, she then showed Tiffany a handful of mud.

"What are you doing? I'm wearing a velvet shirt. Do you know how much this costs?" she asked, pressing her fingers against the fabric.

"A million bucks?" Chrissy said like she didn't care. Then the slimy, brown stuff slammed across Tiffany's face, dripping onto her shirt.

"I hate you!" Tiffany shrieked and charged at her, landing on top of Chrissy in the mud.

They sloshed and rolled in it, ripping and tearing anything they could get a hold of. Their hair soon looked like clay and their bodies like they were dipped in dark chocolate.

Craig watched in amusement. To him, it was like a pay-per-view mud wrestling show and he had front row tickets. Still, he kept an eye on Todd, just in case!

It all seemed to end too soon. Chrissy and Todd had their sweet revenge, while Surla witnessed nothing. They decided to let her rest, and even during the sleep-over, Chrissy did not mention the occurrence. So, you can understand Surla's surprise when she came back to school Monday, seeing Craig with a black eye.

FOURTEEN

After Friday night, Craig and Tiffany demonstrated their exaggerated lust for each other openly, in an attempt to upset Surla. In the hallways, the cafeteria, even outside the library, hands were roving and tangoing tongues taunted her.

The next day in History class, Tiffany bragged to Surla and whoever else could hear, that she and Craig were going dressed up in matching costumes for Revere Park's Halloween bash. "It's going to be perfect."

"Are you going?" Surla cleverly changed the topic to Todd.

"No, I can't," he responded. "I have to take my sister out trick-or-treating. It's her last year of going door to door, so I know she'll want to stay out until way past her bed time."

That information made her feel in a bummer mood, so she tried to focus on the lesson. The teacher was speaking about pirates. It was interesting enough. "These bandits of the sea were ruthless, often taking treasured possessions from other ships by force. They stole anything of value, gold and even food. Ships sunk from firing cannonballs and sword fights ended by death."

She imagined for a second, Craig arriving at the Halloween party as a pirate, his black eye hidden with an eye-patch. *The rude attitude that goes with the costume wouldn't have to be an act and Tiffany could be his squawking parrot. Mmmm, a parrot,* Surla licked her lips subconsciously.

For the period of time that Pussface snuck away from Cathy's, the scrawny cat roamed the dark streets and alleys without any namable reason. Why didn't he go back to Idis? He wasn't sure himself. He just knew he felt confusion, and eating scraps from tin garbage cans didn't help him think clearer.

A few other hungry and homeless felines crossed paths with him, most of whom were punks fighting over basically anything: rebels without a cause. Pussface imagined what they would look like if they were human. They would have super-spiky Mohawks and fake leather pants. Instead of switchblades, these cats had switch-claws.

Hoping for a little refuge and romance, Pussface peeked through a typical hole in a backyard fence. "Why am I even doing this?" He watched Diamond prance around flower beds, chasing little flies. One blue moth in particular seemed as if it was playing along and thinking 'catch me if you can'! It even loopdy-looped and landed on her nose a couple times.

"Hey, Peeping Tom Cat," a deep and lazy voice said from behind Pussface.

He turned to see Lenny, another black cat. (Remember, all black cats can talk, with a witch or without.) Lenny was surrounded by three of his buddies—two were skinny, showing ribs, their eyes big with hunger and the third was an orange and white fat cat.

"What do ya boys want?" Pussface spoke with a tough accent, which comes out whenever he aims to sound threatening.

"We was wonderin' whachoo were doin' lookin' at our Cat Woman." Lenny stepped closer, his posse following closely behind.

"Your Cat Woman? Who says she's yours, Batman?" he joked. "And what's up with Garfield here? Has he been swiping everyone's portion of fish bones?"

Like a trigger, Lenny and the posse's front right claws shot out.

Pussface flinched, arching his back. "Come on now, why does there have to be this black-cat-on-black-cat crime?" the cornered and now scaredy cat pleaded.

The orange cat moved forward, like it was a personal invitation to hurt Pussface.

"This isn't fair. It's three against…" He stopped suddenly, hearing someone coming down the sidewalk. It was a midnight jogger. Not wanting the guy to suspect anything weird, Pussface continued to act like a normal cat until he disappeared around the block. "Hiss! Hiss! Meow! Hiss!" was followed by flailing of paws and spitting.

Lenny and the posse looked at each other with amusement. "That wuz pretty funny, wuzn't it?"

Pussface's snaggletooth poked out in his grin. "Does that mean you're gonna let me go?"

"No." They cornered him, still intimidating him with their razor-sharp switch-claws.

"Wait, I have an idea." Pussface thought quickly. "Let's have a contest."

"What kind of contest?" They were skeptical.

"You know, to see which one of us Diamond would go for."

All their claws retracted with thought. "Yeah, what do we gotta do?" Lenny asked.

"We each have to go hunting for the best present to give her. Whichever gift she enjoys the most, then whoever caught it will win."

"So, you mean like catchin' a mouse for her?" Lenny was warming up for competition.

"Yeah, you got the idea." Pussface's muscles relaxed. "We'll meet back here in twenty minutes. Sound good, boys?"

"Okay, but no cheatin', loser. I better not catch you with her until we're all here and ready," Lenny warned, and then took off down a dark road, with his posse following closely behind.

Pussface once again peeked through the hole in the fence. Diamond was still fervently chasing flies. He almost forgot time was ticking, absorbed in his admiration for her.

The other cats were seeking rodents in a dirty alley. Many rats were skittering around through garbage.

"This will be easy." Lenny crouched down, singling out one that was fat with light brown fur. Its eyes were black and beady; its tail was long and scaly with scabs. Not noticing it was being snuck up on by its worst enemy, his long pointed and twitching nose sniffed at an old jelly donut with hunger. Before it could take a nibble, the black cat had it in its paws.

"Bring over the tray of goodies!" Lenny meowed to his three obedient alley cats. The lid to a tin garbage can was slid over in a hurry. Already laying lifeless on it were three rodents.

Right before the twenty minutes were over, Lenny entered Diamond's backyard with his tin platter.

"Ha ha! We're here first. I wonder if the loser gave up." He strutted toward the white-as-cotton kitty, the food being pushed along by his buddies. Diamond backed herself up into a corner of the wooden fence.

"Hey, we ain't here to cause no trouble, miss. I just came to bring you a gift. A very tasty one. See, these four rats were caught in only fifteen minutes. I'm givin' 'em to you."

Lenny leaned to the feast, snagging by the tail a half-hairless rat with his teeth. The carcass wagged to and fro as he stepped closer to Diamond. "Here, take it. It's for you," he mumbled through a clenched jaw.

The rat was held only two or so inches from Diamond's face. The foul odor, which could almost turn the air green with its stench, seeped up through the kitty's nostrils and suddenly, without warning, she puked. Her Fancy Feast cat food came out in chunks all over Lenny.

"Eeeew!" The black cat dropped the dinner and looked down at his now orange-colored fur. Diamond took that moment to run to the flowerbed and lay low.

"Come on, boys, quick! Let's head to the Smith's; they have a swimming pool." Lenny was utterly disgusted by the incident, and so was Diamond.

Yes! I'm here first, Pussface thought, until noticing the smelly gifts sprawled next to the garbage lid. "Where is everyone? Oh no, maybe Diamond actually fell for the sleaze. I'm a lot better looking than he is! But of course, I wasn't here on time." He sighed deeply, looking around the dark yard, which was illuminated by bright foliage.

With head down, he sulked away, then returned with a brown paper bag in his mouth. A light was flickering from within, and he set it in the middle of the grass.

After Pussface left, Diamond approached the glowing bag curiously. With a paw, she carefully opened the top. Yellow glimmered out and across her pale fur. Inside, the bug's wings fluttered and its body lit up like a light bulb.

FIFTEEN

Idis's Victorian house appeared like a big green monster in the night. Pussface approached the habitation with fear running its chilling fingers across his spine.

Peering through a window, the black cat witnessed Idis on her knees in the center of the living room. Long and black drippy candles burned around her.

The atmosphere had a strange, red haziness about it, while the witch chanted over and over in an unknown language, raising her voice louder and louder. Once she reached the level of yelling, a soft wind twirled around her, ruffling her dress and messing her already wild hair. Suddenly a ghostly being seeped through the floorboards and floated above her like a mist.

"Yes!" Idis cackled, throwing her head back dramatically.

"Oh no. Idis has gone too far." Pussface jumped off the porch, heading in the opposite direction as fast as his four legs could take him.

A scratching from Cathy's bedroom window was so distinct that it woke up Surla. "What is that?"

The black curled up body at the bottom of the bed stirred. "What?"

Scratch... scratch. "That!" she whispered loudly.

"Probably the tree." Cathy was half asleep.

Scratch... "Hey!" a voice called from outside.

"Can your tree talk, too?" Surla pulled the bed sheets over half her face in fear.

"No. Not like your mirror can."

"Didn't you hear that?"

"Hear what?"

"A voice say—"

"Hey!" It finished the sentence. "You, guys, let me in!"

"Oh my gosh!" Cathy's fur stood on end.

"Go away, tree!" Surla said.

"It's me—Pussface! Please, I need in!" They finally had the courage to look at the window where two orange orbs stared in at them.

"Yeah right. I'm not letting you in!" Surla sat up with anger and so did Cathy.

"No, but, but you don't understand. I need to talk to you! Idis is up to no good..."

"Like we didn't know that already," Cathy retorted.

"I'm on your side now, Surla. I always was, except the scaredy cat in me made me listen to Idis. You have to trust me."

"Should we trust him?" Cathy asked, being gullible by nature.

"No way! What if Idis is hiding next to him? And as soon as I open that window, she comes flying in like a banshee."

"Then we're doomed. You're right."

"I don't know how I can prove it to you, Surla. I just wanted to get some refuge and warn you at the same time. "

"Warn me of what?"

"Idis. She is dealing with Black Magic now. I saw her myself, summoning evilness. Now you know that's the one commandment the Witch's Coven holds the firmest—to not deal with Black Magic."

Surla and Cathy turned to each other with wide eyes.

"Why would I lie to you about something like this?" His voice cracked with sincerity.

"Well." She slowly approached the window and gazed through it at all angles. "Okay, cousin… I'm trusting you."

Early the next morning, a little, yellow car pulled into Idis's driveway. Out stepped a small Chinese woman in a long red trench coat. Her heels click-clacked up the creaky porch steps. She then rang the doorbell, which chimed a slow low tune. From inside her coat, something wriggled around and she held the bundle tightly as she heard footsteps coming to answer. Anticipation was evident as she pursed her lips.

The witch opened the door a crack. Dark baggy circles formed around her eyes from the night before, making her already piercing pale green eyes even more piercing. It almost hurt to look straight into them. "What do you want?" Her big nose pointed suspiciously to the concealed object in the woman's coat.

A sickened frown quickly appeared. In a strong accent she replied, "I believe I've found Surra."

"What?! Speak clearer!"

"Surra, your pet. Is there a reward?"

"Oh! Surla! Hurry up, hand her over!" Idis's long skinny fingers reached out. "Finally those stupid posters paid off."

The Chinese woman undid a few buttons revealing the tired black body.

"A poodle!" Idis screeched. "A poodle!"

"Yes. Not Surra?" The runny eyed, curly-furred dog was then held out, and it yelped.

"No, not Surrrrra!" she mimicked in fury. "Surla is my cat, not dog." Idis grabbed a flier and pointed to the crayon picture.

"Oh, it rook very much rike a poodle," she disagreed. "See, short tail and froppy ears."

"You wanna see a poodle? Here!" Her arms shot straight out, fingers stretched and spread. POOF!

"Bye, Mom, I'll see you later tonight." Surla slipped out the door, allowing Cathy and Pussface to follow. It was Halloween night. It was pretty easy to decide on a costume this year. Surla wore a black body suit, nylons, cat ears, and a long tail. Two real black cats and a gorgeous girl wearing a cat costume attracted so much attention walking down the sidewalks, that even little boys running around in Ninja robes looked to each other with dropped mouths.

The three headed toward Idis's. None of them spoke a word to each other until they were standing in front of their spooky destination. It sat there, silent and repelling.

"You're sure she'll be gone tonight?" Surla stood, worried, on the dead grass.

"I'm sure," Pussface spoke up. "I heard her talkin' to Gretchen through Vladimirror. Idis can't miss out on The Witches' Ball this year, because Marilyn Handsome will be there, entertaining."

"Marilyn Handsome, really?" Surla's eyebrows raised with interest. "They've been trying to get him for four years."

"Weird," Cathy whispered. The moonlight cast a mysterious orange.

Together, they creaked up the porch steps. Spread in front of the door was a pool of water. Before Surla moved an inch closer, a ghostly, barely audible, voice moaned, "Don't step in a pooooodle."

"What was that?" Pussface leaned his head back to see Surla's fear in her face.

"Don't step in that—puddle," Cathy repeated.

"No, I'm sure it said 'poodle,'" Pussface said quickly.

Surla shook her head. "Whatever. We're obviously hallucinating."

"All three of us?" Pussface's ears twitched.

"Yeah." Surla proceeded, splashing a shoe in the wet spot.

"Ooo!" they heard a faint voice echo.

"Are you going to say we hallucinated again?" Cathy's tail went between her legs.

The question was ignored as Surla grabbed the door's handle. It felt more than cold; it was icy, and it was locked. "C'mon we'll try another entry."

"What's that note say on the door?" Pussface noticed.

"Oh, Idis puts that up every year to scare off the trick-or-treaters." She tore it off and read, "I eat children for breakfast." Then it was thrown into the bushes.

A tall, black-iron fence separated the front from the backyard. A thick oak tree twisted up and over it. Cathy and Pussface slid their lean bodies underneath.

The railing, which resembled spears shooting up in the air, was too thin for any human body to squeeze through. "Be careful," Cathy warned, waiting in the weeds of the side-yard. She saw Surla grab a sturdy branch with both her hands. Surla glanced at her fake nails; their redness glistened in the night. She sighed with worry, then held on tighter as her feet climbed up the trunk. She was amazed at her strength in her legs, but still it was straining. She hopped to the other side with just more than a few inches away from the spear-like points. Once her feet hit ground, the fuzzy-eared headband fell off and she quickly retrieved it.

"Good job," Pussface complimented.

"It was nothin'," she kidded, while fixing the rest of her hair.

Red-brick steppingstones wrapped around the patio. Moss emerged from the cracks, and waving wild grass tried hiding the path. The patio's cement was severely cracked and exotic plants hung above in old pots. A naked statue of a headless woman caught Cathy's attention, as it sat captured with ivy, arms outstretched as if it was yearning for help.

"Pussface, Cathy," Surla called for their attention. Her foot pushed open a plastic cat door. "You two go in and unlatch the window for me."

"Let's go, partner," Pussface said and led the way through the flap.

Surla worked the holey screen off carefully. Inside, a kitchen unwelcomingly greeted them. Black cauldrons of different widths hung above rust-colored counters. Jars were strewn around, holding squishy, pod-like things with tentacles. An awful smell like an old corpse filled the room.

Cathy gave out a couple kitty-coughs. "I couldn't have imagined it worse."

"If you think this is bad…," Pussface wiped a cobweb off his whiskers with a paw, "you should visit *my* witch's house."

They heard a tapping come from the only window, now without a screen, and saw Surla mouthing to them, "Hurry up."

They jumped to the windowsill, being careful not to tip over a jar full of whatever. A latch was pushed up by the two, making it possible for Surla to slide open the glass and climb through.

"If I'm right…," Surla pulled in her velvet-sewn tail, "the Spellbook should be upstairs in the library." She waved a hand in front of her nose. "Woo! Hurry up. I almost forgot how bad it smells in here."

They went through swinging double doors.

A familiar scene of Idis clipping her toenails on the green couch flashed through Surla's mind as they passed the living room. They ascended the winding mahogany staircase. Reprints of Picasso's early paintings of women lined the wall in the upstairs hallway. Not one depicted a beautiful vision of women.

Surla stopped a moment, like she had done numerous times before to study over one portrait: an exaggerated nose almost jumped off the canvas, red hair framed the sullen face and a frumpy green hat sat atop. Surla remembered Idis posing for Pablo Picasso in his creative, and messy studio.

Surla didn't know a lot of the newspapers, which were strewn around his studio, were actually used in his artwork; she thought the Spanish guy was being so friendly to line the room with poopypaper for her, until one day she ruined something that was very important. Then Picasso yelled at Idis, "Your *estupido gato* has ruined my masterpiece!"

It was a long process to finish the well-known Idis portrait, yet in it she remains nameless. The original portrait has been known to hang in San Francisco's Legion Of Honor Art Museum.

The sound of a book slamming to the floor of the library brought Surla's attention back to its sole purpose. She entered the library, situated inside the witch's cap. Pussface and Cathy were already hunting through Edgar Allen Poe sections for the Spellbook. Dust captured colorful moonlight, beaming through tall stained glass and peacefully landing on bookshelves. Cathy climbed those shelves, searching where Surla couldn't reach. Covers were tattered, bindings broken, pages turned yellow with age, and dirty fingerprints dotted most.

After a long while, the chime of a clock was heard from the next room over. They all froze as Surla counted the time to be nine o'clock.

"We have plenty of time." Pussface poked his head from behind a stack of encyclopedias. "Idis shouldn't be back until waaay after midnight."

"But we've searched through almost everything in here." Cathy looked at her dusty paws with dismay. "And look at the mess we've made."

"Then where else could it be?" Surla put her hands on her hips in thought.

"Maybe Idis is smarter than we think. Why would someone place something so important in the most obvious place?" Cathy said.

"She's right," Pussface added.

"Maybe...," Surla bit her bottom lip, "it's in her room. Yeah! C'mon."

New energy came over them as they entered Idis's, two doors down the hall. The walls and ceiling were painted a midnight blue and a red light glowed dimly from a small lamp, casting its hue across a thick black bedspread, which flowed to the wood floor like magma.

Antique perfume bottles with their atomizer pumps decorated a dresser with ornate designs. Vladimirror stood silently next to the dresser, ominously reflecting the three trespassers.

"Is that the magic mirror?" Cathy asked.

"Yes, that's him—Vladimirror. He can probably hear us right now, if he's not sleeping."

"Aren't you afraid he might tell Idis what we're doing?" Pussface reasoned.

"Not at all. He's tired of the old witch, just as I am. Besides, we're friends. Aren't we, Vladimirror?"

He stood there, still silent. "Vladimirror," Surla called again. "It's me—Surla. I'm switched with Cathy, who's down there." She pointed to her body.

Still silence.

"Okay, this calls for drastic measures," she joked. "Mirror mirror, on the wall. Who's the fairest of them all?"

"(Snore!) I wasn't dialing any 900 numbers, I swear." A swirl of colors took over the reflection. "Oh, dear. That's not Idis. Who are you?" His congenial voice was timid.

"It's me, Vladimirror. It's Surla. I was BeSwitched with a girl named Cathy when I ran away. There she is... in my body...and I in hers. Oh, and there's Pussface, of course."

"So, then, why do you look like a giant cat?"

Surla laughed. "It's my Halloween costume. Tonight is Halloween, didn't you know?"

"Sorry, Idis doesn't keep a calendar in here."

"I came to get the Spellbook, so we can switch back. Do you know where it might be?"

"I know she keeps a book under the bed. I'm not sure if it's the Spellbook. It might be a diary or something because she never lets me get a good reflection of it."

"I'll look." Cathy quickly slid her furry body along the wood floor. Sure enough, she saw something square, just a few feet away. Slinking closer she saw the old English script on the cover, but before she could say anything a sharp pain bit at one of her back paws. "Yeeow!" Her head hit the bottom of the bed by reflex. Slowly she slid back out.

"Ouch, Cathy. A rat-trap is hooked to you." Surla carefully removed it. "Idis hates rats."

"I wonder why," Pussface mumbled sarcastically as visions came to him. *Hmmm… they both have big pointy noses, they both smell, and they both like to lurk in alleys at night.*

Surla bent over, lifting the blankets, after Cathy told her of the book she saw—but instead of seeing a book, two glowing, green eyes awaited her from the opposite end. Surla shot up straight like an arrow and gasped.

"Ha! Looking for something?" Idis, standing up also, didn't blink. "Maybe this!" The Spellbook was brought from behind her back. The gold lettering on the cover shined.

Vladimirror went blank, reflecting the backs of Surla's shaking knees and the two cats sinking to the ground, ears flattened.

"Surla, is that you?" The witch walked closer, scrutinizing the whole outfit. "Half cat… Half girl! Ha! Did the BeSwitching only work halfway?"

Instead of giving an answer, Surla glanced down at the Spellbook, which was now held only a foot away. Like the cat she once was, her body pounced at it. In a millisecond both she and the book were out the door and down the hall.

Idis shrieked, and within the next second the house's whole atmosphere morphed. It gave Surla a severely claustrophobic feeling, as if she were being sucked into a black hole. The place looked as if it were spinning. She dropped to the floor, taking hold of the stairway's banister with her free hand. Her breath was short and panicky with desperation as she saw Idis exit her bedroom, the door automatically slamming behind her.

Idis had an odd calmness about her as the sickening twirling continued. "You aren't leaving this house with the Spellbook… And you might not leave with your life either." Her wretched smile increased.

"You've got it wrong, Idis." Surla pulled herself along the railing. When she reached the top step, she exhaled with relief as the spinning stopped.

"You think you're going to actually win." Idis talked like a concerned mother, whose child had been led astray. "I raised you from birth, I gave you a home, and what do you do to show thanks? RUN AWAY!"

The once sturdy mahogany wood beneath Surla started to crumble.

"Aaaaaaaaaaah!" Surla took hold of the banister, dropping the Spellbook, which made an echoing thud at the bottom story. She attempted to monkey-bar her way down the railing, but they started to snap in half in a domino effect all the way down the winding staircase. Not being able to descend fast enough, Surla fell to the bottom floor, still clenching onto a broken rail.

Upstairs, Pussface and Cathy were involved in a plan to help Surla. Vladimirror was dialing up Gretchen. Out of a green swirling fog, the fat witch, holding a glass of wine, answered, tipsy. "Who has disturbed my par-ty? Pussface?"

"Yes. Please, you gotta help."

"Help what? What's the matter?"

"Idis. She's downstairs right now, trying to kill Surla who's been BeSwitched with Cathy here."

"She is?"

"Not only that, but she is going to do it with the help of Black Magic."

"Black Magic!" Gretchen gasped. Her wine glass dropped and shattered on the ground. "I can't do this alone." With a slight pause, she turned around to her party scene. "Sisters! Marilyn!"

Idis's arms outstretched, and as if being supported by someone under the arms, she flowed effortlessly from the upstairs down toward Surla. Her boots finally came to a clank against the wood flooring. The witch leaned over Surla's weary body. Surla's lungs heaved for breath. Idis loomed over her without expression, then retrieved the Spellbook, and came back to slap a cold, bony hand across Surla's cheek, and laughed. Surla spit at the witch, and it landed in her eye.

"You vile little... ER!" Idis stormed, and a powerful rush of wind thrust Surla against a wall and into a bathroom.

The door slammed shut and locked by itself. Surla's eyes darted around and landed on a window. She slid the clear shower-curtain to one side, and stepped into the old-fashioned bathtub, to open the possible escape-route. She could hear the kitchen sink run with water. Without warning, the bathroom sink's faucet burst out with water, followed by the tub's.

Surla worked at the window but it was no use; the lock automatically went back down with each attempt. "My gosh. This house is completely possessed!" With that said, the shower curtain grabbed at her, enveloping her in the plastic. She tried to fight back, punching and kicking, but it wrapped around each of her limbs with ease, then shoved her down onto her back, water rising around her.

Upstairs, eleven maddened witches flew through Vladimirror, all having very extraordinary characteristics. One that looked the youngest, around twenty-three, had silver long hair which waved into curls at the backs of her knees and blood-red lips that were naturally glossy. "Saffron, where's Marilyn?" Gretchen turned to her and asked.

"He's coming." Her violet eyes twinkled with animation.

"Hurry up!" Gretchen saw him. His long black hair was sleek, skin was pale, and one eye was baby blue while the other was black.

"As long as I don't have fun." He stepped his gangly legs through the mirror.

"They're downstairs fighting. It sounds like it's coming from the bathroom," Pussface quickly informed.

Idis was in the kitchen washing out her eye, when the witches snuck toward the swinging doorway and peeked in. "Go check the bathroom," Gretchen ordered Marilyn.

"Idis." Gretchen threw open the doors, with the sisters close behind.

Idis turned around and her eyes now literally glowed. "What?! What is this?!"

As Marilyn walked to the bathroom, he heard clanking of pots, shattering of glass, and shrieking coming from the kitchen. He turned the bathroom's doorknob and it unlocked. Inside, he saw Surla under water, weakly struggling. Slowly, he walked over to get a better look. Surla's eyes were pleading. Air escaped her mouth, making little bubbles surface, and her hair waved like silk.

Emotionless, Marilyn said, "Let her go." With that order, the shower-curtain released and water stopped rushing.

Surla sat up, choking for air. Before she could speak, he was out the door, heading to the kitchen. She squinted her eyes in thought.

Cathy and Pussface leaped from the upstairs to the green couch downstairs. They soon saw Surla dripping wet, ringing out her fake tail, exiting the bathroom.

"Hey!" Surla rushed over to them. "What's going on in the kitchen?"

"We called Gretchen up for help," Cathy said.

Inside the warzone, Idis seethed with evil. Her hair twirled around like snakes. She stood on a counter throwing anything not attached to the ground by her magical powers. The witches danced around, arms waving, collecting their own magical powers together.

Gretchen, prancing on her fat feet, noticed Marilyn studying a jar of goop. "Hey!" she said breathy. "Whose side are you on? Help us!"

He looked up momentarily, then continued, studying another jar. The air had a magnetized feel. Their skin was tingling with the sensation. Gretchen, Saffron, and all the other witches knew what that meant. It was the feeling of evil powers fighting good. Idis's Black Magic was just as strong as the eleven witches all together. With every step-ball-change they danced, they felt weaker, until most hunched from over-exertion. Evil was now overcoming good.

From between the floorboards, Idis summoned black demons, which looked like nothing more than shadows with red eyes. Eleven demons seeped in to overtake eleven witches.

Surla peeked into the kitchen long enough to behold a demon slither through Saffron's lips. Her back arched, lunging her chest forward while her neck rolled. Her once violet eyes were now red and the color beamed out like lasers.

"It's terrible." Surla shut the door and ran to her friends. "What can I do? I can't use my magic unless I'm back inside my body."

"Oh my gosh!" Cathy gasped. "Is that the Spellbook?" Her paw pointed to the fireplace mantle.

Surla jumped, overcome with joy. "I can't believe she left it out here!"

"We'll finally be switched back!" Cathy saw some dust fly when the heavy book was set on the couch next to her.

Surla flipped through as fast as she could, ruffling and ripping pages as she went. "Hurry," she told herself. "You'd think it would have an index." More and more ruffling. "Ah! I think I found it! Here it is. Okay."

Cathy and Pussface leaned over the page. Its title read, "BeSwitched Back." Their hearts pounded with excitement.

Once again, Surla was short of breath. "Cathy," she wheezed, "do you have asthma?"

"No." Cathy twitched her right ear. "Just calm down."

"Relax," Pussface interjected. "Take deep breaths."

Surla closed her eyes, tilting her head back. "Okay." She looked back down to the spell and began reading. "If you did not take heed to the Black Cats' Rule, events have taken speed to pay your toll. So you say you are ready to be once again thee…"

Just then, the doors of the kitchen flew open, interrupting the magic. Idis glided on a foot of air, leading twelve possessed witches, and three demons without a body.

Panicked, Surla looked down to the spell, trying to find where she had left off, when suddenly, from out of the fireplace, Idis conjured a massive fire. Its red and blue flames grew and flailed out, giving off tremendous heat. Idis laughed hysterically and the witches echoed her cackle in deep voices.

"The Spellbook please." Idis smiled and automatically the old cover slammed shut on Surla's fingers and was pulled by an unseen force to the fire. "Now that I have this incredible power, I don't need that old junk anymore. And you know what that means, Surla; I won't be needing you anymore either." She turned, facing her back to them, as she enjoyed watching the hungry flames eat at the spells.

"Get out of here Surla and Cathy," Pussface said quietly. "The front door is right there. Run away as fast as you can."

Surla turned to Cathy and then back to Pussface. "But… but now what?"

"Listen, I have a plan. A really good one. Now if you don't want to be overtaken by one of those demons, you better get the heck outta here," Pussface continued.

Quickly, Surla grasped Cathy in her arms and quietly exited through the front door. The crackling and popping of the fire made it impossible for Idis to notice.

As Surla ran down the dark, wet streets, she cried, holding Cathy tight. She thought of the couple of weeks before, when she had first jumped through Idis's window and over a hydrangea bush, calling out, FREEDOM... FREEDOM AT LAST, in her head. Cathy mewed sorrowfully, bumping and shaking, with every step.

Energy disappeared without notice, making Surla stumble on a sidewalk and fall to the concrete. She wasn't hurt and neither was Cathy. They just laid back together against a stone wall. Finally finding time to wipe away tears, Surla used both of her forearms. "I want to be me again," she whimpered.

"So do I." Cathy's yellow eyes were moist. "I don't care how boring my life is, just as long as I have my life."

"I agree. And I don't like human boys."

"But I do."

"And I hate that stuff called pizza, although the anchovies weren't bad."

"My favorite food."

"What about driving. I would much rather roam and wander on my paws."

"I'm supposed to be getting my license soon."

The longer they disagreed on likes and dislikes, the dryer their tears were, while their faces became long with the realization that they were never going to be back to themselves.

Soon they heard loud music. The sadness had drowned out any sound earlier. "You hear that?" Surla sat up and straightened her cat-ear headband.

"Yeah. It's called The Monster Mash." Cathy's tail stood up. "Oh, how I wish I could dance right now."

Surla picked up Cathy and stood to see. They were actually next to the small, segmented stone wall, which wrapped around Revere Park. Guys and girls, dressed scary or exotic, filled the park. A set-up stage was placed at one corner and a banner read over it—Washington and Jefferson High's Halloween Bash.

"Cathy!" they heard someone call. It was Todd, walking over to them from a refreshment stand. "Hey, I was hoping you would come." He leaned in and gave her a warm hug, then scratched under Cathy's chin. "Hey, it's Psycho Kitty." He smiled, showing off his cute dimples.

"I thought you weren't able to make it." Surla worked on fixing her hair as she spoke. All that fighting made her look pretty messy.

"My sister went trick-or-treating with her friends." His green eyes looked over her now holey stockings, to the tight black body suit, and landed on her sparkling eyes, which now had mascara runs. "Are you alright?"

"Uh, not really," she admitted. "But where's your costume?" She eyed his black T-shirt, which fit tight around his chest and upper arms.

"Oh, I didn't have one, so I just came as myself." Todd said, as he watched Surla's eyes widen with sadness. "Do you… wanna dance?"

"No… not really."

At Idis's, Pussface was sitting at the kitchen's open window, meowing an alarm to all the other black cats in the town. "Rrrreeeooow! Rrrreeeooooow!"

The witches and demons were still standing in the living room, as a vortex sucked from the center of the floor. It looked like a black whirlpool of gases and tar.

As the vortex bubbled and grew, dozens of black cats were scurrying through the kitchen window and cat door. Even Lenny showed. "I'm here to help, too," he said to Pussface. "That fight I had with you over Diamond was stupid. I'm sorry it had to happen, man, cuz I know she doesn't like me anyway."

"Hey, it's okay." A crooked fang poked out when he grinned. "Help me siren."

Soon the kitchen became so full and black with cats, that many were balancing on hanging pots. Pussface said, "I think we're ready."

When they entered the living room, three possessed witches had already stepped into the vortex, disappearing. Gretchen, still possessed, almost stepped in, but stopped when Idis finally noticed all the cats surrounding her and the demons. "Ha, now what's this?"

All the felines hissed at once, showing their sharp teeth.

"You think you all could defeat me?!" She cackled.

Hooking tails, they were involved in a choreographed spell. The circle, first going clockwise, turned suddenly, hooking tails with the partner to the right of them, continuing counterclockwise, rolling their heads and sticking paws in and out of the circle.

"Get these foolish cats out of here!" Idis ordered the demons. The witches mechanically spread out, and their laser-red eyes didn't blink once.

Gretchen's overtaken body was heading to Pussface and Lenny, when suddenly, all the cats clustered together. Their fur combined, along with their tails and eyes, into one giant black cat! "You are going to need a bigger demon, to possess this body." Pussface's voice came through two foot-long fangs.

SIXTEEN

Tiffany walked by Surla, pulling Craig's hand. She was dressed as a mermaid in a long, green and sparkly dress. "Oh my gosh. Look at Cathy. What happened to her?" She laughed and continued on her way.

"I think I'm gonna go home now," Surla said to Todd, turning to walk away.

"Wait." He put a hand on her shoulder, but she didn't stop. He kept by her side at the same pace. "Come on, Cathy. Don't go yet. I want to talk to you. I don't like to see you so upset."

"Listen." Surla's feet stopped. "I-I just wish I could have my problems go away. But, now, no matter how hard I try, they won't go. I'm going to stay like this forever.

"Stay like what?" His eyebrows raised.

"This is who I am for the rest of my life."

Cathy buried her head in Surla's arms after hearing that.

"What's wrong with that? I like who you are." His eyes were filled with concern.

Surla's eyes started to tear up again. "This isn't who I am."

"Cathy." He reached an arm around her shoulders. "Come sit over here."

He led her to an open bench, which was far from the whole party-scene and underneath a maple tree. Cathy sat on the other side of Surla. "I want to tell you, that I think you are the most beautiful girl, even with runs in your stockings and your hair messy." He smiled. "Tiffany isn't half as beautiful as you—that's why she's so jealous. And Craig—he's just a jerk who was stupid enough to let you go."

Cathy's ears were straight up, focusing on every word. Surla just sat there, being polite, her eyes sometimes wandering up to the starry sky.

"Even before this change you've had the last couple of weeks," he continued, "I saw something inside you—so special, so sweet."

Cathy felt something inside she never felt before; she felt special and wanted. The feeling of loneliness escaped her and just at that moment she saw something in the sky, which Surla noticed, too. "A shooting star." Surla smiled at it briefly.

"I wish… I could make you feel better." Todd said softly. And right when the star landed, he kissed her.

Surla felt a tingling, supernatural sensation—and so did Cathy. Then suddenly *Cathy* felt a warm set of lips on hers and she opened her eyes instantly, seeing Todd's eyes closed in pleasure. She was involved in a kiss with Todd!

As they continued to kiss, memories embedded in Cathy's mind, from Surla's experiences in her body, flooded in like a stormy ocean: visions of bumping into him in the hall; smelling his cologne; receiving help in the library after school; riding home with him and first realizing how strikingly good looking he was, with his perfect dark hair and beautiful cheekbones, with those lips and eyes. With every memory, the kiss became more passionate. Cathy felt his smooth face with her hands. Then the horrific night at the lake surged in: lightning and thunder and the feeling of being stranded in the cold, rainy night—only to wake up in Todd's arms helping her inside his truck.

When their kiss parted, Cathy held him close, in awe and utter amazement. "Wow, I'm me again."

Todd laughed, taking that as a huge compliment. "That *was* magical."

Surla was busy rolling in the cool grass in pure joy.

The melody of a slow song floated to their ears. "Shall we have that dance now?" Todd asked.

Cathy wrapped her arm around his and held hands as they approached a small clearing between many other couples.

Surla trotted around in happy circles, then jumped onto a chair near the refreshment table. She watched Cathy with her head on Todd's shoulder, smiling with closed eyes as they danced. Once in a while he would lean in and kiss the top of her head or say something in her ear; then she would either smile or laugh and look into his eyes.

Tiffany soon came over to the table. Craig was by her side, dressed as a pirate, covering the black eye with an eye-patch. Surla laughed inside. *What a dumb costume.* She eyed the striped pants with disgust.

"Are you sure you don't want any more?" Craig asked Tiffany, filling his plate with many snacks.

"Yes." Tiffany's blond tendrils sparkled with hair spray glitter.

Hey, I have the use of my magic back, Surla thought, curling her tail in delight. "This spell is directed to Tiffany," she whispered. "You will dread tomorrow and today, because the opposite will be said, for what you really wanted to say."

"All you had was a cookie." Craig was persistent. "Do you want some punch?"

"If I had anything else…," Tiffany said defiantly, "then I would be fatter than a whale. I am on a diet." Her eyebrows quirked. "Er!" She fought what she was saying. "I mean…, why do you think I wore this long dress anyway? It's covering up my… Uh! My fat legs."

"Sorry, I was just asking." Craig set down his plate. "Let's dance instead." He walked her to a spot right next to Cathy and Todd.

Tiffany stared hard at the two. Finally she uttered, "Cathy is so pretty... and look at what a cute couple she and Todd make."

"What?" Craig loosened up his hold around her waist.

"Did I just say that?" Tiffany looked up at him in disbelief.

"Uh, yeah."

"What I meant to say was, I wish you danced like him. You are a terrible dancer."

"No I'm not." Craig let go of her completely.

"I-I really mean it. No! I mean, um, you just can't dance!"

People looked at her, having heard the last loud comment, including Cathy. "Dance alone then." Craig walked to the closest available girl. "Would you like to dance?"

"Er!" Tiffany bit her tongue.

"Yeah right, Craig. I hear you leave your dates in the woods," the girl's voice trailed.

As Cathy and Todd were nearing the end of the slow song, Chrissy rushed over and flashed a picture with her camera. "High School memories." She smiled.

"Hey, cute costume," Cathy complimented the flapper-girl dress.

"Thanks. Well, I'm gonna go take a few more shots of people." She started walking off, then turned suddenly, "I told you he liked you!"

Screech! The song ended with the microphone on stage making a piercing noise. "Sorry 'bout that." The Dracula D.J. laughed. "Well, as the night has gone on, it has given our judges ample time to decide on this year's costume contest winner!"

Cheering and clapping showed the excitement from both the student bodies.

"Father Townshend..." He turned to the P.E. teacher dressed as a priest. "May I have the envelope please?"

Mr. Townshend grabbed the mike. "Yes, my son, but first you must repent."

"Repent of what?" Dracula went on.

"For sucking neck with my niece tonight."

"Woooo!" Guys cheered from the back and more laughter waved through.

"You should be grateful, Father." The D.J. had a sly look to his fake-blooded smile.

Hooting and whistling started up.

"Oh, and why is that?"

"I helped make her more... holy." He opened his mouth, showing off the fake fangs.

"Hahaha!" Cathy laughed out loud with everyone else.

"May I now have the envelope?"

"Yes, my son, just don't get too close to me."

"Why not? Are you afraid?"

"No, I have really bad garlic breath tonight."

"Ew! That would be very offensive." He drew his cape up over half his face. "Hurry and hand me the envelope."

Mr. Townshend did, then bowed and waved at the applauding crowd. "And the winner is... Wait, no drum roll?"

Already planned, a guy dressed in his band costume came up on stage with his drum.

"Great! Great! Come over here."

Marching, he went over to Dracula.

"Now give me your drum."

Acting confused, the guy reluctantly handed over the drum, then offered his drumsticks.

"No, no." Dracula refused the drumsticks. "Now for the drum roll."

Everyone cheered and waited. Surprisingly, he bent down, placing it on its side, then gave it a push. It began to roll across the stage and people cheered and laughed more. "And the winner is, the lovely, Tiffany Randall as a mermaid!"

Smiling brightly, she climbed the stage's steps, then stood in front of the mike, as the D.J. handed her a bouquet of orange carnations.

Her eyes sparkled, her hair sparkled, and her sea-green dress sparkled. The crowd grew silent, awaiting her thanks for winning.

"Uh hum," she cleared her throat, seeing the many faces in front of her, some masked. "I guess I'm supposed to show gratitude for winning this thing, but, uh, it was easy! I mean, well, look at all of you. Your costumes are pathetic. None of you know how to dress, even when you're out of costume. What are you supposed to be?" she reluctantly said to a heavyset boy, wearing all white. "The Doughboy?" She bit her bottom lip as most everybody gasped. "No, I-I didn't mean that. I meant, a chef, or a-a marshmallow." Tiffany covered her mouth.

"What is she doing?" Cathy looked up at Todd, who was just as shocked. "Ah, jeez! I am so dumb." Noticing that echoed out across the park, she put the mike behind her back as a reflex.

"You *are* dumb!" a guy yelled from the crowd and people yelled out comments in agreement.

Surla quickly recited another spell aimed for the most embarrassing thing to happen to a human being.

Tiffany felt her abdomen rumble. Then, without any way of turning back or holding in, a sound came out like a motorcycle revving up, but with more oomph. She, you know, "cut the cheese," "let one go," and it horrifically amplified out from the microphone for everyone in the audience and neighborhood to hear.

"Ew!" the audience yelled. Instantaneously, a couple of car alarms started blaring out from the parking lot. Tiffany dropped her carnations. Orange petals dotted the black stage as she stood there frozen from shock, her eyes as wide as a fish.

Suddenly, from a nearby street corner, a fire station bell rang out like a scream. Cathy and Todd busted up in laughter and disgust, like everyone else.

Soon rushing over, with its flashing lights and yellow firemen, a fire engine stopped in front of the park.

"Everyone, clear out!" The men ran, carrying heavy hoses, hooking them to hydrants. Tiffany finally ran off the stage, and out of sight.

"What's going on?" Cathy asked, seeing all the frantic people.

"Clear out! Can't you smell that?" a red-faced fireman called to her and Todd.

"Huh?"

"There's a fire." Todd pointed through to the other side of the park. "Right there! See?!" Flames billowed up and white smoke filled the dark sky. "Let's get out of their way."

He grabbed Cathy's hand and jogged, leading her out to where all the cars were lined up against the sidewalk, along with the fire truck at the red-zone and soon an ambulance came. Many partiers were gathered out there with them, watching with excitement.

"Todd," Cathy said, looking into his eyes, "isn't this the second time you've saved my life?" She placed her arms around his neck.

Before he could answer, she had him involved in a kiss. He didn't want to ruin the moment by telling her the fire must have been fifty yards away, out of harm. Instead, when they parted, he asked, "Can we pretend I saved your life for a third time?"

Chrissy ran over and snapped a picture of them in each others' arms. "That was perfect! Isn't this one crazy night? I wonder what started that fire in the first place."

Faster than expected, the fire was out and paramedics were called over to help. Three men, two carrying a stretcher, and one holding first aid supplies, ran out to the burned area.

"Oh my gosh. Do you think there is a body out there?" Chrissy continued. Everyone else was thinking or saying the same thing.

"I hope not!" Cathy gasped.

Surla was sneaking around the wheels and taped-off area where only the firemen were allowed.

One big man, with a curled mustache, was sitting as the driver for the ambulance. He was talking to a lady officer. "Yeah, some guy, Lenny, called the station a couple minutes ago. Boy, he was right on time. A minute later and these flames would have really spread."

"Why are they calling the paramedics out there?" The lady officer strained to see. "Someone's hurt?"

"I suppose." He was just as surprised as she. Spectators came as close as possible to the ambulance without being a nuisance. Todd and Cathy happened to be in a section of the crowd that had a good view of what was happening.

Soon the back doors of the ambulance flew open and a stretcher was being propped inside. Cathy caught a glimpse of what looked like a charred broomstick poking out of the zipper to a body bag.

SEVENTEEN

A police car sat on the curb outside of Idis's. At the front door, a lady officer talked with a Chinese woman who wore a red trench-coat. "So, what you are trying to tell me is, you were suddenly transformed into a… puddle?"

"Yes! Crazy Americans. I tell Gramma 'bout this one. First prane to China!" Two dirty shoe-prints marked the back of her coat as she scurried off into the night.

The officer put out her fist to knock on the door, but it creaked open on its own. It was Marilyn, but he was different now. His black hair was combed back into a neat, small, ponytail. His eyes were a pretty gray-green, and even more, his whole Gothic wardrobe was gone. He stood there in a preppy striped sweater-vest and beige khaki pants. "Hello." His voice was rich and smooth. "What can I do for you?"

"Well," she started. "I got a 'disturbance of peace' call and …," she paused from what was about to be said, "a spinning house. Can you tell me of any strange occurrences that may have happened in this house?"

"Now I'm going to tell you the honest truth here." He rubbed his chin in thought. "All I remember is, one day I was having a drink with a very attractive and famous woman. We were getting very drunk," he continued, "and woo! She told me she was *like* a virgin…"

"Yeah." She had no idea where this story was headed, but her eyes showed obvious curiosity anyway.

"So, of course I was very taken by her. I mean, this very attractive woman was interested in me and I remember she looked deeply into my eyes and said that I must be her lucky star. Then, in the next moment, I am a huge rock star and my name isn't Marvin Manson—it's Marilyn Handsome."

"Uh huh." The officer was still interested, but said, "What's it have to do with tonight?"

"I'm getting to that part." He smiled and leaned an arm against the door-frame. "Well, life as a rock star was not what I thought it would be like. It didn't make me happy. I dreaded the word 'fun' and hadn't cracked a smile in four years. All I remember about tonight is… I was turned back to my old self."

She laughed in response and said, "Well, now that you aren't a famous rock star anymore, what do you plan on doing?"

"Oh, I'm going to Disneyland!"

She heard the seriousness in his voice but laughed anyway. "Is there anyone else here I can talk to about tonight?"

"…Other than twelve possessed witches, I don't… Wait, the witches are already gone."

She laughed some more. Then the sound of metal clanking caused Marilyn to turn toward the inside the house. "I guess there *is* someone else here."

Dressed as a knight, a man with brown, long hair took off his helmet and greeted Marilyn and the officer. "My heavens, I feel splendid."

"Interesting costume. It looks very authentic," Marvin said.

"That's because it is authentic, my fellow. The name is Vladimir." He extended a hand to them both, one at a time. "What a great night."

The officer then began to question him for her report, but he had nothing to offer except to say he wasn't a 'mere reflection' of anyone else anymore.

"So, I don't understand. Why would I receive a disturbance of peace call? You two seem like very well-mannered men."

"I don't know..." Vladimirror worked his heavy armor off, to which he now bore a delicious physique.

Marilyn answered, "Maybe it was all the cats meowing."

"It was probably a prank call then, 'cause why would someone see a spinning house anyway, unless they were watching The Wizard of Oz."

"Wait, actually, this does look like the back door." Marilyn pointed out the plastic cat-door. "And where's the driveway?"

Within the next couple of seconds, they heard a motor start, then a yellow station wagon sped from the backyard, to the front and down the road.

Vladimir cut into the perplexing moment by saying to the officer, "Do I know you from somewhere?"

"I, uh, don't think so. But your voice sounds very familiar." She worked on putting a loose strand of curly hair back under her hat.

Slowly, he reached his hand forward and pulled off the hat. Out plummeted a mound of beautiful blond strands.

Quickly, Vladimir's eyebrows raised in realization. "Cindy?"

"Uh, yes," she said, confused.

He then said, "Cindy? 1-555-Cuff-Me?"

She blushed and Marilyn stood there silent, looking at the two in curiosity.

"Well, I guess I've got my report." She arched an eyebrow.

"Hey, why don't I escort you to your car."

She accepted, and as Vladimir opened the driver-side door for her, he added, "I always keep your number on redial."

"How long have you been interested in police procedure?" Marilyn heard her say.

EPILOGUE

What's going on in each of the characters' lives:

Pussface, after setting Idis's broom on fire and sending it through the sky like a shooting star, became a hero. He still had to go back and live with Gretchen, which he doesn't mind. The relationship they had was much better than Surla and Idis's. On occasional visits back to Cathy's town, he still pursues Diamond, and thinks she will finally come around.

Tiffany hasn't been seen at school since the embarrassment she made of herself at Washington and Jefferson High's Halloween Bash. Chrissy says she still sees her come out of her house to get the mail. Right at this moment, Tiffany is working with a tutor in the privacy of her own home. She's on Independent Study.

Craig hasn't been able to get a date in months. The news spread around school about what he did to Cathy on their date, and now girls don't even want to look at him. Right now, he's spending a Friday night home alone, watching Jeopardy with his mom.

Chrissy had the pictures developed from the party. She decided to sign up for Journalism next semester, so she could help write and choose photos for the yearbook. The one of Cathy and Todd dancing will be placed right next to the one of Tiffany dropping her carnations with mortification in her eyes. Right now she is laughing for her hundredth time about that night.

Marvin Manson did go to Disneyland and had a blast riding Space Mountain over and over again. He has written a book about eating sushi with meditation and it will be released next June.

Vladimir has been seeing the officer, Cindy, for the last couple of months. They aren't interested in a serious relationship; they're too wild and flirtatious for that (give him a break, he's been a mirror for the last couple hundred years). It turns out, he is interested in the entertainment industry as well. Right now he is tearing off his shirt for a wrestle-mania championship.

Surla is still best friends with Cathy and she hopes it will last forever. She can be found lying on the porch with her two other friends, *Pussface* and *Diamond,* on sunny afternoons. Lately, her thoughts have been on the deeper meanings of magic and the influence it has had in her life and others'.

Cathy is still with Todd. She became homecoming queen and is thinking about being a veterinarian some day. All she wanted in her teen-life is finally piecing itself together. Right now she is brushing her hair in front of her mirror, which is plastered with pictures of her and Todd at different events together.

Todd became homecoming king and is thinking of becoming a pro football player. But if that doesn't work out, he wouldn't mind being a professor of Chemistry. He has stayed madly in love with Cathy since the night of the Halloween party. Right now, Todd is on his way over to pick up Cathy for another date.

Idis was brought to the morgue on the night of the Halloween party. The coroner could have sworn he saw her big toe twitch. Right now, Idis is...

THE END

ABOUT THE AUTHOR

Molly Snow is a Top 10 Idaho Fiction Author, awarded by the Idaho Book Extravaganza. Her works include quirky teen romances *BeSwitched*, *Head Over Halo* and *To Kiss a Werewolf*. Also a speaker on writing, her school assemblies have been featured in *The Contra Costa Times* and *The Brentwood Press*. Snow is married to her high school crush, has a set of silly twin boys and a bobtail cat named Meow-Meow.

mollysnowfiction.blogspot.com
breezyreads.com

Made in the USA
San Bernardino, CA
17 March 2014